# SCANDALIZE
# MY NAME

# SCANDALIZE
# MY NAME

*Fiona Sinclair*

*with an introduction by*
MARTIN EDWARDS

This edition first published in 2025 by
The British Library
96 Euston Road
London NW1 2DB
bl.uk

For product safety information, please visit
shop.bl.uk/pages/british-library-publishing,
or the Publishing pages on bl.uk.

Cataloguing in Publication Data
A catalogue record for this publication is available from the British Library

ISBN 978 0 7123 5547 6
e-ISBN 978 0 7123 6804 9

Original cover image: *To Victoria Embankment*
by Ralph & Brown Studios, 1928.

Image © London Metropolitan Archives (City of London).

Text design and typesetting by Tetragon, London
Printed in Scotland by Bell & Bain Ltd

# CONTENTS

# INTRODUCTION

*Scandalize My Name* was the first novel published by Fiona Sinclair. The book's appearance in 1960 seemed to mark the start of a career rich in promise. In Paul Grainger, Sinclair introduced a likeable Scotland Yard detective who investigates a neatly crafted mystery full of well-drawn characters. Grainger has a good deal in common with another detective who made his debut two years later; this was Adam Dalgliesh, created by P. D. James.

There are a number of coincidental similarities between Fiona Sinclair and P. D. James and their early work. There is no doubt in my mind that they are indeed coincidences, but they seem to me to be so striking that I'm tempted to wonder whether the author of *Scandalize My Name* might have been capable of achieving as much success as the woman who wrote *Cover Her Face*.

Tragically, however, that question can never be answered, because Fiona Sinclair died the year after her first book appeared. In all, five of her novels were published, three of them posthumously, but her early death meant that her work in the crime genre was soon forgotten.

This is sad, since although there are aspects of *Scandalize My Name* that display the author's inexperience—for instance, she introduces a large number of characters very quickly, and is overly fond of shifting viewpoint within short scenes—there are plenty of indications that this was a writer with a genuine talent for storytelling. Most important of all, the novel remains a good read more than sixty years after her death.

The book begins in a hurry. The first chapter introduces a host of individuals with reason to dislike Ivan Sweet, and by the time it comes to an end, the victim has met his inevitable fate. From the start it is clear that we are in the hands of a capable writer with a neat turn of phrase; on the very first page, we are told that from Ivan's "basement redoubt his personality had invaded the house, gently, imperceptibly, touching with leprous fingers".

One of the hallmarks of a skilled crime novelist is an ability to write with authenticity, so that the reader is willing to suspend disbelief when confronted with the elaborations of a twisting plot. The description of the post mortem in the third chapter—which is unflinching in a way that is now commonplace, but must have seemed ahead of its time in 1960—demonstrates Fiona Sinclair's command of detail; her husband Michael Peters was a pathologist and the medical backgrounds in her writing always carry conviction.

We are introduced to Superintendent Grainger and his Scottish sidekick; Sergeant McGregor has come to realise that his superior, a pipe-smoking Oxford philosophy graduate with a lean aristocratic figure and a "scholar's stoop" is "a fine fellow to work for". During the course of the book, we learn that Grainger is thirty-eight years old; he is a widower, having married sixteen years ago in a "war-time wedding". His methodical approach to the investigation is reflected in the way he makes a careful list of suspects, with comments about motive and opportunity, in a manner reminiscent of Golden Age detectives. But it is his understanding of human nature that eventually enables him to discover the truth about the murder of Ivan Sweet.

Fiona Sinclair was a pen-name. She was born Fiona Maud Baines (not Blaines, as some sources suggest) in 1919, and in her younger days she appeared on the stage. The biographical note on the dust jacket of the first edition of this novel said: "her stage training has been unexpectedly useful. 'I can lean back in my chair and listen to my characters talking to each other, which helps a lot,' she explains. As a young actress she studied the Stanislavski method, which has also assisted her in her building of character, for under this method the actor or actress has to imagine the past and the future of the character he or she is playing." She was an attractive and charismatic woman who had, in the words of her son Roderick, "a luminous presence".

I first came across her work when I acquired a first edition of this novel, which she had inscribed to someone called Martin; I gather that he was a colleague of her husband Michael and a close friend of the couple. The book was accompanied by a letter from Michael to friends in which he said, "We were going to throw a party to celebrate but unfortunately she's in hospital." However, Sinclair (as I'll call her, to avoid confusion with her daughter, also Fiona) did have the pleasure of seeing her first novel in the front window of a bookshop close to her home in Highgate.

*Scandalize My Name* was well-received, and Michael's letter noted a couple of reviewers' plaudits, in the *Evening Standard* and *John o' London's*. *Books and Bookmen* was equally positive: "New author Sinclair brings an unexpectedly assured and professional touch to her first attempt at the traditional form of detective story."

Like Adam Dalgliesh, Grainger is a widower, a cerebral fellow who lives alone in a London flat and still bears the scars of bereavement. Both detectives are sensitive and humane, intelligent and determined. Like Fiona Sinclair, P. D. James was married to a doctor, and both women's lives were touched by extreme tragedy; James's husband suffered from mental health problems, and died in 1964, while Sinclair's life was devastated by breast cancer.

Grainger returned the following year in *Dead of a Physician*; this book, unlike her other novels, was published in the United States, under the title *But the Patient Died*. Set in a hospital, the story benefits from Sinclair's understanding of medical life as well as procedures, notably brain surgery. The novel, which in some respects anticipates James's *Shroud for a Nightingale* (1967), was described by Jacques Barzun and Wendell Hertig Taylor, the notoriously acerbic co-authors of *A Catalogue of Crime*, as "one of the best stories of murder in hospital". Sinclair dedicated the book "to my many dear friends among the Medical, Nursing and Ancillary professions without whose skill and devoted care I would not have lived to complete it". Sadly, however, she died a short time after the book was published.

One of the characters in *Dead of a Physician* is a young doctor called Geoffrey Tremaine. Passing mention is made of an earlier case in Cornwall in which he'd been involved and those events are described in *Most Unnatural Death*, which was eventually published in 1965. The story is told by Anne Carmichael (who has been married to Tremaine for six weeks by the time *Dead of a Physician* opens) and Grainger is introduced only in the latter stages of the story. The manuscript was found among Fiona Sinclair's papers after her death, and the chances are that it was the first crime novel she wrote.

As has often been the case when researching authors for this series, I have benefited enormously from talking to people who knew the author, in this case her surviving children, Roderick Peters and Fiona Hodgson. As a result, I'm able to give much more information about Sinclair than has previously been available and also to correct one or two mistakes to be found in the infrequent references to her in the public domain.

Sinclair came from an artistic and cultured background. Her parents were William and Joy Baines and her father was a successful architect who painted watercolours for pleasure. Her mother came from an Irish family and was even more closely involved with the world of the arts; her circle included Benjamin Britten and Peter Peers. At one point, Joy spent a year travelling with Romany people in eastern Europe; on her return she brought back a gypsy caravan which she kept in the New Forest; Roderick recalls visits to the caravan during his childhood. William and Joy had two children, Fiona and Keith. Keith (1924–84) was a poet and translator; unable to make a living in England, he travelled to Mallorca and was befriended by Robert Graves, with whom he collaborated for a time. On returning to England in the Sixties, he lived in London with the second of his three wives, Janet Boulton (1936–2024), who herself became a well-respected artist specialising in watercolours.

Sinclair became interested in acting, and while still in her mid-teens she appeared in the West End in a production of *Alice in Wonderland*. She trained at LAMDA, the London Academy of Music and Dramatic Art, which is the oldest specialist drama school in the British Isles, but it seems that a combination of marriage, war-time, and small children effectively put an end to any theatrical ambitions she had. A keen horse-rider, she met Michael Peters, who shared her love of riding, in Oxford, where he was studying medicine. They married when she was just eighteen.

A few years later, she was pregnant with Roderick while her husband, who had joined the RAF and became a squadron leader, was out in Burma. This was a very difficult time, but Roderick and his mother would tell stories to each other, and her enjoyment of weaving those stories may have helped to encourage her literary ambitions. When Michael came home, he was in a poor physical state, but strength of will carried him through. In the course of his career, he gave expert evidence in a number of murder trials, and his obituary in 1977 described him as "an outstanding histopathologist". The couple had three children; another son, Roland, died some years ago.

Fiona Sinclair was a highly capable gardener, her enthusiasm perhaps a legacy from spending time at Roast Farm, Saffron Walden, after being evacuated there. She wrote poetry before concentrating on prose, and was personally acquainted with Ngaio Marsh, the New Zealander who achieved success both as a detective novelist and as a theatre director. It is conceivable that Marsh encouraged Sinclair—who also enjoyed the books of Agatha Christie and Dorothy L. Sayers, as well as the work of Daphne du Maurier—to write crime fiction, or perhaps she was simply been inspired by their success.

However, in 1956 she was diagnosed with breast cancer and a long period of medical treatment and operations began. Roderick believes that the illness, and the uncertain prognosis, spurred her on to write: her creative powers were formidable and she felt driven to achieve as much as she could, despite her illness. The family lived in an exceptionally tall house on Highgate Hill, with views of the North Downs on a clear day, and at every opportunity Sinclair worked on her fiction in the attic room at the very top of the building. It seems likely that she used her own home as the model for Magnolia House in this novel.

Something extraordinary happened after Sinclair's death, explained in Sean Day-Lewis's memoir of his father, who was not only the Poet Laureate but also (writing as Nicholas Blake) an accomplished detective novelist. In *Cecil Day-Lewis: An English Literary Life* (1980), there is reference to a lecture, "The Golden Bridle", given by the poet at Harvard in 1965, in which he discussed the inspiration for his poem "Elegy for a Woman Unknown". Michael Peters and his wife had admired Day-Lewis's work for many years, and after her death, Michael Peters approached him and showed him the poetry she'd written. Day-Lewis didn't believe that the poems were publishable, but he was greatly moved by the story of her suffering, her courage, and her early death. While staying on the island of Delos, he came up with the idea for the poem, which remains as a permanent memorial to the impact that she made, even on those who never met her.

A happy outcome of this connection was that a friendship developed between the Peters and Day-Lewis families. Both Roderick and his sister Fiona remember spending time with them and visiting the poet and his wife and young son Daniel in Greenwich.

Two more books featuring Grainger were also published posthumously. *Meddle with the Mafia* appeared in 1963; Fiona Sinclair loved Italy and she and her husband spent time there in the last year of her life. It was followed by *Three Slips to a Noose* (1964). Her early death makes it difficult to be sure about the order in which she wrote her books, and whether those that were posthumously published were merely drafts rather than the finished article. Perhaps she suffered rejections, perhaps she wanted to hone her skills before submitting her work to the public gaze.

Whatever the precise sequence of events, I think that had she lived, and benefited from skilled editorial input, she possessed the range and ability to develop into a major crime writer, perhaps similarly to Mary Kelly, another author of quiet accomplishment whose books have been republished as Crime Classics and whose interest in character was a notable feature of her work.

We'll never know. But I do know that I find Fiona Sinclair's personal story poignant, as is her poem "Bequest", written towards the end of her life; and I'm very glad that her family and the British Library have agreed to include it as a coda to this reprint of her debut mystery. As for her crime novels, they are well-written and entertaining and I believe they are unquestionably worthy of revival.

MARTIN EDWARDS

www.martinedwardsbooks.com

# ONE

THE HOUSE HAD STOOD UPON THE HILL FOR NEARLY THREE hundred years; even before Wren's St. Paul's rose in its splendour of new white stone upon the skyline, it was there, the many windows in its rose-brick walls looking out towards London. A London that had now long since engulfed it, taking the meadows and the home farm and all but one cottage, but leaving the great house bulked above a walled garden that still retained the fragrance of an earlier time. Foursquare across the hill-top it stood; its mighty roofs supported by carved white modillions; its tall windows, wearing here and there a round wrought-iron balcony like a diminutive crinoline, looking down upon the roaring traffic that thundered up the hill as once they had gazed upon nervous galloping horsemen urging thudding hooves up the slope.

Caroline, too, stared out at the restless traffic, her mind's eye revolted by the memory of Ivan Sweet's pale cold face and the explosive malice that had seethed behind his dead brown eyes...

It had all begun with such deceptive quietness when he took on the basement flat nine months before; he had been quietly persuasive, well mannered, undemonstratively enthusiastic. And Naomi had spoken so warmly of him. Yet from his basement redoubt his personality had invaded the house, gently, imperceptibly, touching with leprous fingers.

Oh God, how can I go through with this party tonight, knowing he's there, she asked herself, and turned restlessly from the window. She stared, unsoothed at the great drawing-room, warm with summer sun and scented with roses and it came to her with a new shock of horror that she no longer belonged in this peaceful room. She had become a stranger in her own house.

A rustle sounded at the door and she turned to see her daughter Elaine in a shimmering blue-green gown.

"Oh, Mother," said the girl, "I've been looking for you. Could you do me up please?"

Caroline Southey hooked the tight-fitting dress across her daughter's warm, fair-skinned back; the girl's white shoulders and slender neck rose out of the gown to bear a graceful head of dark red hair. How young her flesh is, thought her mother, and how perfect; her unsteady fingers achieved the last fastening and she said:

"You look wonderful."

Elaine smiled happily, "It does suit me, doesn't it?"

She looked down at the shining silk, swinging her hips a little to see it move. Caroline stared at her as she stood there glowing in the evening sun and all her fears welled up afresh. Oh God, she prayed, dear God, she's innocent. Don't let her be hurt. Don't let harm come to her through us!

"I have such a strange feeling tonight, Mother, as if something absolutely tremendous were going to happen. Isn't it silly?"

Caroline's smile felt stiff on her lips.

"No, love, of course not... come, we must hurry."


William Southey frowned as he tied his black tie for the third time. He was a tall, dark man with a wide forehead which receding hair had made still larger. He wore a small pointed beard and a black velvet dinner jacket, but he did not aim at the conscientiously flamboyant and the face reflected in the mirror was unselfconscious and austere.

He rose rather wearily and began to put away his paint-stained working clothes; his wife's gown was laid out across their double bed and for a moment he stood looking down at it. A painful sadness came in to his face and he rubbed his broad painter's hand across his forehead as though to push away the thoughts that lay beneath the bone. Macbeth's words thundered across his mind 'What's done cannot be undone'. But the moment passed. I'll be damned if I want it undone, he thought and Ivan Sweet's face faded slowly from his mind like a receding nightmare.

He could hear his wife's voice now from the adjoining room where she was speaking softly to the baby and a moment later she came in. They exchanged a brief strained smile.

"Shall I help you into your dress?" he asked.

"Thank you, Will." She stepped into the gown and stood still while he fastened it. Automatically William's eyes registered the slight familiar figure, the soft, wavy hair, greying now; and the sense of unreality deepened. As he finished their eyes met in the glass and for a moment he saw clearly in her face the girl he had married more than twenty years ago.

But Caroline sat down suddenly as if she were very tired.

"I do wish Richard would come in," she said. "It's not like him to be so late for Elaine's party…"

"I expect he's with Yolande… He'll be in soon. How's Elaine?"

"Radiant!" She busied herself with cosmetics, frowning a little before saying awkwardly, "Will?"

"Hmm?"

"She's in a dream… on top of the world… I would like her to have as much of tonight as she can without a shadow on it…" Their eyes met and Will nodded.

"Of course I'll do what I can," he said. He smiled suddenly, "Our little redhead, twenty-one and lovely as the day…" He stopped abruptly, his head raised to listen.

"It's all right," said Caroline quickly. "It's Richard."

"Hallo, Dick, you're late," called his father and the boy's voice reached them from a distance.

"Oh hell! I won't be long."

"You shouldn't be unkind to that boy, Yolande, he loves you." Henry Meade sighed at the mutinous look his daughter gave him and took out his old-fashioned gold turnip watch, holding it away from him so that his long-sighted eyes could read its face.

"You must get ready, my love. Already we shall be late for Elaine's party and that is more than discourteous in these days of inadequate domestic help."

He kissed the top of her head, a long, thin man with a Victorian dome of a forehead over a gentle melancholy face; a relic of a generation soon to be lost, liberal and humane, self-disciplined and unashamedly pedantic.

Yolande turned from the window of their Georgian cottage and looked unhappily at her father. She remembered with a momentary surprise how the things they had done together had seemed to fill her whole life—until she met Ivan. But now her world had shifted its centre and was taking on new colours and new patterns. It was time the old fogey brought himself up to date a bit, Ivan had said impatiently; why should she live like a museum piece? And yet… life with Ivan was sometimes rather alarming… As for Richard Southey, well it was really very silly of him to hang about when she had told him she and Ivan were in love and going to get married.

Standing all the distance of his sixty years away from her, Henry regarded her perplexedly.

"Come, dear, have your bath and put on your pretty frock," he said.

Yolande's eyes came to rest on his face again and stayed there, startled. Despite his gentle tone, something was in his face that sent a cold shudder of fear through her. Perhaps he noticed it, for in a flash all strangeness was gone and his aspect so familiar that she could only believe herself mistaken and foolish.

"I'll be quick," she promised. But she hesitated a moment and laid a hand on his arm, "Daddy?"

He smiled at her questioningly.

"Daddy, couldn't you try to like Ivan?"

Immediately she wished she had left the words unspoken. The unfamiliar, cold impassivity seemed to freeze his features again, and his arm was stiff under her hand. After a moment he replied carefully,

"I won't be picking any more quarrels with that young man of yours. Now off you go."

"Can't you make that damn brother of yours fork out enough to go on with, he's always throwing money around though God knows where he gets it from. He seems to be out of work as much as he's in it."

Phoebe struggled with a dress for which she'd grown a good deal too plump, as she threw the question at her husband who sat on the unmade bed leaning against the bedpost, gazing at her abstractedly. A small child in a cot watched them solemnly; in a basket on a trunk in the corner, a baby was sleeping.

"Ivan won't part, you know that." He began to roll a cigarette. "Southey's an influential chap; I suppose he might put some commercial stuff my way if I asked him. I'll think about it if nothing else turns up."

"Nothing will turn up. If there's any hope in that quarter, for Heaven's sake ask him tonight when you see him."

"A good fifty other people'll be seeing him, too."

His wife made an exasperated sound.

"Oh, well, all right, I'll see how it pans out. If that damn sitter-in doesn't get here soon, we won't get there at all tonight."

"You shouldn't be rude about her considering she does it for nothing." Steps sounded on the bare stairs outside their one-room flat. "There she is now."

Patrick Sweet got off the bed; a small, dark, restless young man, tense and on edge despite his effort at a lackadaisical manner.

"You there, duckie?"

"Come right in, Mrs. Haggis."

"Didn't like to march in on you, case you was dressin'. My, don't you look a treat! Y'ought ter dress 'er up more often, do 'er good," she remarked to Pat Sweet, her tone carrying an undercurrent of disapproval.

"Naow, you run along and 'ave a good time. We'll be as snug as a bug in a rug, won't we, dearie?" she apostrophised, the small face peering at her through the cot bars. "Say bye-bye to Mum then."

Out in the street husband and wife started the long climb from the slums at the bottom of the hill to Magnolia House at the top.

★

From her secret peephole in the hedge of Magnolia Cottage, Theresa Jonas stared with an intensity of envy at the big house; the tall windows, with their rich hangings, bowls of flowers, occasionally frames for the family scenes within, filled her with hard restlessness. She sought in her small shrewd mind for words of denigration to ease the pressure of her hate. Sometimes this was effective, but at others she played with the idea of flames, merciless flames licking the smooth panelling, devouring the shining silk, reducing the proud house to a pile of smoking rubble. Or if some calamity of disgrace...

"Theresa, Ther-ESA!" her mother's shrill, irritated voice made the girl jump. She looked anxiously down at her party dress and crept round to the kitchen door, keeping in the shelter of the hedge; she knew from experience that the downstairs lavatory could give her an alibi.

Upstairs in her dreary bedroom Barbara Jonas sat at her mirror, applying make-up without art to a sallow complexion and struggling with greasy dun hair. In the small bathroom near by, Edouard (meticulously pronounced for the distinction his French name was felt to confer on the family) hummed a dance tune as he brushed his hair. A narrowly built man with rather pretty good looks, he enjoyed a party where a little trivial flirtation could be carried on surreptitiously under cover of the general jollity. If it attracted his wife's censure, well, that was nothing very new. He brought out a pair of nail scissors and trimmed the small neat moustache above his small neat mouth.

"Edouard!"

"Coming, dear."

"Aren't you ready yet?" she asked. "That girl's disappeared and she's probably ruining her dress in the garden. Send her up to me, will you?"

Edouard squinted ruefully at his half-trimmed moustache in the mirror before he obediently turned to go. Somewhere downstairs a door shut.

"Oh, there she is. Thank goodness for that. Well, you can make the boiler up, and then you'd better feed the cat. Tell Theresa I want her."

When the girl came in her mother subjected her to a long scrutiny. She was a tall lanky child of thirteen, almost completely lacking in any natural grace of posture and movement. Her protuberant eyes were of a cold pale blue and she had her father's small pretty mouth, slightly disfigured by a tendency to projecting teeth. Her light brown hair might have been pretty but it was drawn back over-severely into tight plaits. She simpered now under her mother's stare, but receiving no response began to feel scared and drooped disconsolately as she waited for a rebuke.

"Hold yourself up, child!" Barbara's tone had a hint of savagery in it; her objective study of her daughter had precipitated an unwelcome comparison with the Southey girls. Her inward resentment was flared against them. Suppose, she thought, Ivan had already… she pushed the thought away and stood up, smoothing her own oyster-coloured dress over her thick hips. She wasn't fat, but short and stumpy, only about an inch taller than her daughter. As their eyes met, something in the child's crushed look made her feel compunction and she pulled the girl to her in a sudden rough embrace.

"Now get your coat and wait downstairs. Tell Daddy to come up, will you?"

When Edouard came in she looked at him hard and said:

"You'd better be careful how much you drink. It would be unwise to become too talkative."

★

"Your supper, Mr. Paignton."

Cecil Paignton put down his razor, rinsed the soap off his face and carefully dried it. He folded the small towel with precision and replaced it under the basin. The sight of his bare neck in the mirror distressed him and he reached for the collar and tie on the chair beside him, then remembering the woman waiting at the door, he was flustered and crossed quickly to take his supper tray.

"Sorry to keep you waiting," he said, unwillingly appeasing.

"Well, if it's cold, I can't 'elp it." Mrs. Jarrow stared at him with horrid interest. Cecil flinched under the regard of those cold, pale eyes; he felt particularly vulnerable without his collar and tie—he wanted to cover his throat with his hands.

"Well, I must give Jarrow 'is supper." The landlady creaked off down the stairs whence the smell of cabbage drifted up. Cecil closed the door with relief; he resisted the temptation to lock it—he'd feel a fool when she came back for the tray.

His mind revolved ceaselessly in anxious circles as he tied his tie and brushed his thinning hair to meticulous neatness; should he go to the party, or shouldn't he? Did anyone believe those unspeakable aspersions of Sweet's? Would anyone throw them up at him? Could he manage to laugh as if it didn't matter?

He ought to go, yes of course he ought... his thoughts scattered like frightened sheep but soon he found them again huddled together in the familiar pen; the unspeakable injury that Ivan Sweet had done him had undone the work of years, frustrated a triumph that would have been the justification for all this indignity... His eyes roved the room again, resting with distaste on the sordid tray by the window—even the drinking glass dirty as usual, he noticed with disgust.

But now it's over, he reminded himself. I must cease to be upset by Ivan Sweet or all will be for nothing... it's part of the past... the past.

On a sudden surge of confidence he settled briskly to his supper. Just a part of the past... like a talisman he repeated the phrase as his mood showed a tendency to ebb... a part of the past, a part of the past. Carefully he brushed every speck of dust from his dark blue suit and his trilby hat. He pulled on his gloves; at the door he looked back, his slippers lay pigeon-toed where he had slipped them off. He returned and placed them neatly side by side under the bed. He took a pipe from the rack on his desk, but, about to put it in his pocket, his hand stopped uncertainly. Carefully he replaced it in the rack. He habitually performed small acts of self-denial in the hope of buying good fortune from fate. And so armed he set out for the party at Magnolia House.

In the turquoise bathroom of her attic flat high up under the roofs of Magnolia House, Naomi Moore stepped out of her scented bath. It was hot up there under the old tiles on this summer evening and the casement was opened wide in the dormer window. As she slowly dried herself Naomi idly watched the steam drifting out, hazing the view that stretched away beneath her far over London to the distant Surrey hills.

She sighed as she slipped on her housecoat; she was very tired and felt unequal to the effort of the evening ahead. But I can't afford to be tired yet, she thought; it's essential that I'm at that party. She stood there, frowning unconsciously, while her mind wandered back into the day and abruptly slid off again. She was so still that a pigeon, its breast rosy in the sun, strutted unconcernedly along the wide leaden pathway, the seventeenth-century equivalent of the meagre modern gutter, that ran only a few feet below her window. At last she walked briskly into her bedroom and settled herself at her mirror. Her long, well-kept hands moved over her make-up tray picking out cosmetics and applying them with the ease of long practice. The familiar routine soothed and calmed her. Random thoughts sprang up here and there in the calm, like weeds between flagstones; I should have realised, she thought, that Ivan was a man born to disturb. Perhaps any man so attractive to women was likely to prove—disruptive. She remembered other men who had also been attractive… she caught sight of her own face in the mirror with unbelief… this smart but ageing woman in the glass, could it really be herself? Had it all come to this, the years of her power over men, her all-preoccupying enjoyment of them—and theirs of her? Her husband had been dead for nearly twenty years now and no children had lived… a vivid memory took possession of her without warning, the baby daughter who had died before she was a year old. Where would I be tonight, and what manner of woman, if she had lived, Naomi wondered now? Oh God, but I'm tired. I must get away from all this soon. She shuddered, thinking of that night not long ago when she had woken in the small hours, half stupefied with gas and had just managed to stagger out on to the landing before she collapsed. And only a few days later, she had taken a fall down the long curving flight of stairs from her attic flat. She was only bruised and shaken (even as a child she had had a talent for falling without harm); but she realised now as she looked ruefully at her face that the fall had taken it out of her. She rose wearily and took a dress from her wardrobe; I must go downstairs now and play my part at the party, but after that I'll get right away from here.

*

The light, spacious hall of Magnolia House faced the walled back garden and rising from it the great stairway curved its way upward through the house. Below it an inconspicuous, locked door concealed the entrance to the basement stairway. Beyond this door the bright daylight that flooded the upper rooms became a luxury. But space and grace remained; there were no more curled fronds carved in the wood, but the stairs were shallow and of a pleasing curve. They descended into a wide, tiled passage off which were two shadowed but well-proportioned rooms, a well-equipped kitchenette in what had once been the walk-in pantry, and right down at the end of a tortuous passage, a bathroom which, with its old, barred window and gay pastel tiles seemed an intriguing graft of an Ideal Home on a dungeon. The twilight rooms had been furnished for their tenant by the Southeys, but it was evident that Ivan Sweet's personal tastes did not coincide with the exuberance of the Southey home. Among the Regency stripes and gilt light-fittings, his own bleached and functional possessions stood out; one or two curved chairs with gawky broomstick legs, some low white metal furniture, an Anglepoise lamp, its long neck twisted to throw light on the ceiling, and a few pale pictures whose network of lines contrived obscenity. It was rather as though a crop of surrealistic toadstools had moved in to decorate the basement in their own fashion. The whole flat was meticulously tidy; there were no open letters, no photographs, no scorched pipe and bulging pouch, none of the comfortable small disorder of the man who lives alone.

Only one thing was out of place. Significantly so. This was in the bathroom where Ivan Sweet lay, slim, pale-skinned and dark-haired, his towel warm on the bathrail. His slippers awaited him on the thick mat, his pornography convenient to his gaze on the chromium bathrack. All this comfort availed him nothing however, for the tepid water had filled his lungs and now idly lapped his forehead as the water still gently flowed from one tap and dripped in a slow stream over the bath's edge, while about him the old house vibrated to the merciless traffic on the hill outside.

# TWO

J ONATHON BLAKE LOOKED UP AT MAGNOLIA HOUSE AS HE
beat a vigorous tattoo on the knocker. To his surprise, the
door swung open, and he found himself staring down a long,
cloistered passage running along the wall of the house, lighted
by open brick arches green with creepers. His feet echoed on
the stone and he found himself in a garden enclosed by high
brick walls.

The sound of voices and laughter floated out from the house
and finding the door open he wandered through it, fingering
his collar uneasily as he realised he was late. A small girl with
an obvious resemblance to Dick greeted him demurely and he
started upstairs. At the top there was a rustle of silk and a shim-
mer of turquoise, and he caught sight of a girl whose bare white
shoulders and russet hair gleamed in a shaft of sunlight from the
tall landing window. He stopped dead, his eyes feasting unashamedly. She turned and caught sight of him standing rooted on the
stairway and at that moment, as though Aphrodite had leaned out
of the past in a burst of music, from somewhere high up in the
house the strains of Handel's 'Where'er You Walk' rose on the air
and floated down the stairwell towards them. The lovely liquid
sound, the simple perfection of the singing phrases clamoured at
their ears and they both stood still while the golden sound poured
relentlessly on:

Where'er you walk, cool gales shall fan the glade,

Trees where you sit shall crowd into a shade,

Where'er you tread, the blushing flowers shall rise,

And all things flourish where'er you turn your eyes…

Caroline, on her way to the drawing-room, saw them and stepped back into shadow, all her anxieties fading for a moment. Across the room William felt his heart contract. It's a long time since Caro looked like that, he thought; Oh God, where will this tragic tangle end?

Cecil Paignton, his foot on the bottom stair, blinked without comprehension at the two young people who blocked his way. The boy was nice-looking, he noted vaguely, and promptly forgot the thought.

"I say, do you think we could come up?" asked a small girl's voice with a hint of impatience. And the moment was ended.

Elaine smiled and said in her soft-textured voice:

"What's your name? I'm Elaine Southey."

Jonathon had reached the top in three bounds. He took her hand.

"How do you do. My name's Jonathon Blake, I was up at Cambridge with Dick."

Elaine's eyes were on the hand that held her own, a big hand with broad finger-tips and a dusting of fine red hairs along the back and up the wrist. Feeling unwontedly shy, she raised dark blue eyes to his, only to lower them again to hide the tremor that ran through her as his bright hazel gaze met hers.

"May we come by please?" The voice of Elaine's young sister sounded again behind them and they both laughed; the elder girl moved forward, beckoning Jonathon to follow her into the big drawing-room, her whole body aware of him walking just behind her.

"Jon! Jolly good to see you," exclaimed Richard, detaching himself from the crowd as they came in. "Elaine, this is Jon Blake who was one of the big men at Trinity when I was a freshman, now boning up on leachery at Guy's. All right, old chap, you needn't knife me!" he answered Jonathon's furious look, "I said *lea*chery, not lechery."

Elaine laughed at the young man's distraught face.

"It's all right, we're all hardened to Dick's impossible sense of humour," she comforted him.

Across the room Naomi Moore sat gracefully on the wide window-sill, a half-filled glass of wine in her hand. She was looking up with flattering interest at the big bearded man who boomed like a bittern above her.

"So you hope to hold an exhibition in the autumn?" she asked. "I am most interested, you will let me know, won't you?" The beard wagged with delighted affability as Gregory Saunders took down her address.

"And this is Rachel, your wife." Naomi looked up at the big black-haired girl at his side, her intonation indefinably altered as she continued, "Gregory tells me you are an artist, too."

"I don't sculpt, I paint"—Rachel's voice was almost as resonant as her husband's boom—"in what time is left to me by a four-months' son, that is." She drank down her sherry with enjoyment. This was her first night out since bearing the boy and it was good to be here in a big crowd, in a handsome room, and good to think of Tony's hungry nuzzling and the warmth of his little furry head on the crook of her arm. She would have to leave the party later to get home for the last feed.

"You have a little daughter of about that age, haven't you, Phoebe?" Naomi remarked.

"One of five and one of two months," Phoebe Sweet answered mechanically. William Southey was coming towards them with a tray of glasses and she was anxious to prod her husband into conversation with him; she had managed to pay the milkman that morning only by borrowing from a neighbour little better off than herself. It wasn't easy to enjoy all this luxury when there was so little in the larder for the children tomorrow.

"Her husband's an artist, too," Naomi continued. Gregory looked up, "Oh, what's the name?" he asked.

"Don't worry, you won't know it," Pat answered. He too had seen Southey approaching and realised his wife's intention. With a muttered excuse he moved off. Phoebe looked after him hopelessly.

"Oh dear," Naomi was genuinely put out, "I didn't say anything to offend him, did I?"

Phoebe shook her head, "Of course not, Mrs. Moore. I ought to apologise for him, he didn't mean to be rude. He was out in Korea and he had a head injury. He's been—he's had times like this ever since."

William Southey studied the group by the window, seeing them in terms of light, contrast and colour; Naomi, well-groomed in black, leaning against the window with the confidence of a woman who has always been pretty and successful, flanked on either side by brilliant colour; on her left the full curtain doubly lit by the white gleams of daylight from without and the yellow light from the chandelier within; to her right clustered the large Rachel in her low-bodiced evening gown, Gregory's massive dark bulk and Phoebe's honey-coloured plumpness. Her green dress was too tight. She looked unhappy, he noticed, and it occurred to him that she was Sweet's sister-in-law. He knew the brother only very slightly but he also seemed a very unsatisfactory sort of fellow. As he eased his tray in among the group he thought that Naomi always collected people about her; she had a passion for people and their lives; he remembered how often he had seen her managing them with skill; she was a mistress of the perfectly timed and modulated response, the amused laugh, the naïve compliment, the little remark that unsealed the speaker's next reserve.

"Why so stern on this gay evening, William?" Naomi's light voice roused him.

He smiled, "I was merely thinking what an attractive picture you all make," he answered with partial truth. He changed their empty glasses for full ones and moved on.

Edouard Jonas, obviously a little the worse for alcohol, was trying to flirt with a rather sulky Yolande.

Richard hung about near them, looking very black indeed. Poor Dick, thought William, how they do go through it at that age. Yolande had been a nice child, too, before Sweet got hold of her. Why she should prefer that blackguard to his son was something he could hardly be expected to understand. He glanced at his watch. Nobody appeared to have missed Sweet yet, except Yolande. He himself could scarcely be said to miss the fellow.

He decided that the time was opportune to clear the floor for dancing and asked old Henry Meade to take over the radiogram. Behind them as they sorted records he could hear Barbara Jonas holding forth on Education, and beyond her high penetrating voice the comfortably hilarious roar of talk and laughter rose and fell. He could hardly reconcile the gaiety with the preoccupations jumping and twisting in his mind. The fresh smell of flowers was mingled now with tobacco and wine and spirit, the perfume of the woman guests and the smells of warm silk and cloth. He glanced at Elaine, absorbed in Jonathon and her radiance caught the breath in his throat.

"So far—so good," murmured Caroline to him a little later as they stood drinking and watching the dancers.

And at that moment the music stopped and startlingly clear across the momentary silence came Naomi's voice:

"Ivan doesn't seem to be here yet. He can't have forgotten, can he?"

"I shouldn't think so," replied William dryly, "but his brother's with us tonight. Perhaps he would go down and see." He listened to his own voice with care. It was perfectly steady.

"I'll go," offered Yolande.

"No, love." Henry Meade's voice unusually firm. "I'm sure Mr. Sweet doesn't mind fetching his brother."

"No, I'll go," Pat agreed.

"You promised the next dance to Richard, you know," Henry Meade reminded his daughter quietly when Patrick had gone. He returned to the gramophone and put on the next record, but the sound blurred and he apologised and took it off again while he changed the needle.

Rachel, about to dance with her husband, looked round her curiously, her large shapely nostrils widening as if they sensed menace in the air. What's come over everybody all of a sudden, she wondered? They were like cats on hot bricks when a mere moment ago the party was getting going with a colossal swing; the little chap with the *pince-nez* hanging on his snub nose couldn't look more scared if he was awaiting his executioner, and that ghastly mud-coloured woman with the ghastlier pink daughter looked like a stuck pig, or some regrettable statue, standing there clutching the unfortunate chap she'd landed for a partner. The nice old Victorian effort was mussing his effects, too, that boss shot with the gramophone was surely out of character, he looked a most precise and efficient old bird, and even that elegant woman, Naomi Moore, was looking a little out of true. Suddenly the music started again, and she shrugged her shoulders and got down to enjoying a dance with Gregory; whatever the trouble, it was none of her worry.

Suddenly, as the party once more co-ordinated, abruptly, the lights went out. The electric gramophone slowly lost speed, distorting the music to a long-drawn-out, increasingly bizarre moaning.

"What in Heaven!" exclaimed a startled voice, and someone let out a faint scream.

"It's all right," William's voice was calm. "It's only a fuse. Must be that damn downstairs light." He added to Richard, "Got a torch, boy?"

"There's one in my room, I'll get it," they heard his feet racing up the dark stairway outside. The sound of the baby's crying sent Caroline hurrying off to comfort him. A pale light from the summer night still showed through the long windows and once people's eyes were adjusted to the gloom they began to chatter and laugh rather hysterically. Across the room Edouard took advantage of the dim light for his own purposes and was audibly slapped. His wife glared at him through the half-darkness.

Richard reappeared with a torch and cannoned into someone standing in the doorway.

"Who the devil!—" he shone the torch on the dim figure. It was Patrick Sweet. Richard stared at him in astonishment, his face was paper-white and stirred by a tic. He said with an effort:

"I went down and turned on the light inside the door and it flashed and everything went dark. I—I went on down and called to Ivan, but he—he didn't answer."

"I expect he's out," remarked William practically. "The light just fused, I'm afraid. We'll soon put it right."

"Well, there's a damn queer noise down there."

"What sort of noise?"

Dead quiet reigned in the room as it awaited Pat's reply.

"It was—it sounded like something dripping."

"Looks as if we need a plumber as well as an electrician," Richard remarked, following his father's lead. William gripped the swaying man by the arm and led him to a chair.

"Here, have a drink man!" he said. "I expect we could all do with one." Jonathon's tall figure loomed up in the dark.

"Can I help, sir?" he asked. William paused a moment. "Yes," he answered then, "I'd be glad of your help. Dick and Elaine'll find it easier to cope with drinks in the dark than you would. We'll go downstairs." Their footsteps receded away into the deeper gloom of the stairwell.

Standing in groups in the half-dark, the party guests drank and chattered, but the constraint of waiting lay over them and as the time lengthened the minutes passed more slowly and then more slowly still as, like disease among a herd, silences spread among them touching one group and then another until it was those who spoke who were conspicuous and lowered their voices to whispers. Among these, gathered together in the whispering darkness was there perhaps one—or more than one—for whom this waiting was intolerable, whose heart knocked against the ribs that encased it, whose breath now seemed to burst the lungs that stretched to draw it in, whose belly rebelled against the mind that rode it, whose limbs trembled in the concealing darkness? Was it from here it emanated, the dis-ease that swept the waiting-room?

Without warning the lights returned, and the people blinked and looked pale in the sudden glare and slowly began to talk again until they heard the heavy footsteps gradually ascending the stairs and their voices died away so that when the door opened and William came in, they looked at him in silence and knew that they'd had reason to feel afraid. Caroline went white and swayed as she saw her husband's face, and Richard held her firm with an arm about her waist as they waited for what he had to tell them. With eyes that were dark and shadowed in the hollows of his skull, William looked at them and said:

"I have to tell you that there is a dead man in the basement. The police have been called and will be up here at any moment. No one may leave."

# THREE

IVAN SWEET NOW LAY NAKED ON A TIN TRAY IN THE MORTUARY refrigerator, awaiting his post-mortem. Had his murderer been present in the huge gloomy room, had he wandered round between the high marble slabs, each fitted with its lavatorial drain to carry away the unaesthetic refuse of a corpse, had he considered this ten stone of meat whose secrets must be forcibly revealed before putrefaction and the crawling maggots claimed their own, had he seen the cold white body of his enemy dangling like a horribly overgrown baby in the arms of the mortician as he was heaved on to the slab to be dissected, supposing he had seen all this, would his own thoughts have condemned him? Or had he been provoked so far beyond the bounds of human sensibility as to feel only triumph that he had reduced a living man to meat, bones and a stench?

These questions remain unanswerable, for that invisibly branded individual, the murderer, was not present in the mortuary, and once the hunt is up it is fear for his own neck, more than any horror for his own act that haunts him by night and by day.

Jones, the mortuary attendant now freeing the scalp from Sweet's skull, and Bailey, the Coroner's officer, smoking unconcernedly and exchanging doubtful jokes with Jones, were quite free from any morbid reactions.

"Quite a lady-killer he looks, don't he?" Bailey remarked, jamming his black homburg more firmly on his head as he bent forward to examine the corpse's face.

"Not now he does not," returned the Welshman, as he peeled the dead man's scalp forward over his face so that the hair hung like a sort of freak beard over the chin. He picked up a saw and began sawing off the top of the skull. As the sound of the saw died away they heard a car draw up in the yard outside.

"That's Dr. James's car, isn't it?" asked Bailey.

"'Tis very probable. He's more often early than late, is Dr. James, but we're ready for him, and a good thing too. He's no fellow to appreciate being kept waiting."

"Moves though, don't he? And likes everyone else to do the same. He's a treat to watch though. When you've seen as many as we have you get to know the ins and outs of it. First time I watched one of these, I thought it'd all be over in ten minutes. Must be easy to see what a chap's died of, I thought, if you take a look inside 'im. But, blimey, I had to think again when I had a look in myself!"

"Well, an' after all, it's nothing so surprising, is it now, if you uses your head? How often is it a mechanic can tell you what's wrong with a car the moment he puts his head inside it? An' a car's a man-made thing when all's said and done."

"Good morning, good morning," barked Dr. James, hurling his square bulk across the mortuary and rapidly donning his post-mortem garb. His secretary, a well-groomed, efficient young woman followed him in and finding a relatively bloodless stretch of floor near the slab for her dainty high-heeled shoes, she ensconced herself there ready to take down the pathologist's report. As soon as Dr. James was dressed in his rubber boots, white gown, apron and gloves the Coroner's officer handed him the notes he had prepared. James glanced at them and then at the dead man.

"In the bath, eh? Well, an improvement on hanging yourself from the picture rail, I should say." He raised his eyebrows at Bailey who answered,

"It would be, sir, but we don't reckon it was all his own work; he…"

"O.K.," James broke in, "don't tell me. All down here, I know." He tapped the papers and ran his eyes quickly down the sheets before handing them back.

"Hmm. Anything else I ought to know?"

"Not yet, sir. Natural causes could be the answer, but…"

"But that's what you want me to tell you. Quite."

He walked over to the corpse.

"Could be a coronary thrombosis I suppose, don't know though, looks too young." He flicked the scalp back into position to look at the face. "Hmm, more likely sub-arachnoid haemorrhage if it's natural causes, or a fit, of course. Well, we shall see."

He moved round behind the dead man, wrenched free the previously sawn-through cap of the skull and laid it like an inverted bowl underneath. He then excavated the brain and carried it over to a sort of bedside table projecting over the legs of the corpse, where he explored it quickly but exhaustively with his knife.

"Not sub-arachnoid," he remarked briefly, "quite normal."

He made a slit from chin to pelvis through the white skin with its little patch of curling black hairs on the chest, and deftly removed the breast-bone and rib cage, grasped the root of the tongue and pulled it back through the slit in the neck, clipped and cut the gullet above the stomach and drew out the 'pluck' (lungs and heart with their attachments and the neck structures), placed it on a table and rapidly cut and examined it system by system.

"Hmm, natural causes beginning to look doubtful," he remarked. "No coronary thrombosis here. Hasn't bitten his tongue either, they usually do if they have fits. Drowning's the actual cause of death, of course, but nothing yet to show why."

He returned to the corpse and continued to remove system after system, splitting every duct and vessel, exploring the marrow within the bones, the contents of the stomach and bowels, the inner and outer surfaces of the liver, spleen and kidneys, all the glandular systems, all those wonderfully intricate and finely balanced structures which only a short time before had smoothly functioned to maintain this cold bloody flesh as a living man.

As the pathologist worked, he dictated his findings to his secretary, a string of accurate, unemphatic technical descriptions. He exuded concentration, eyes and brain keyed to detect the subtlest variation from normal; fifteen years of such work had taught him just how subtle an important variation could appear. The job was, to him, no mere dissection of dead matter, but an exploration into the receding mysteries of life itself; although, being English, he would never have described it in such terms.

When the corpse was at last empty of secrets discoverable to the pathologist's knife, he handed it back to the attendant to be made presentable for burial, and was given jars in which he placed the stomach, intestines, liver, spleen, kidneys and portions of the lungs and brain. These he sealed and labelled and handed over to the Coroner's officer against a receipt. It now rested with this officer to deliver them by hand to the Home Office Analyst, whose report on the presence or absence of poison would determine the next stage of the case.

And so it was that Ivan Sweet's organs gave the final verdict on how much someone had hated, and maybe feared, or perhaps envied him.

"Yes, hatred, fear or envy; which will it prove to be this time, eh, Mac?"

Superintendent Grainger laid down the report he had been reading and addressed the remark to his sergeant in his pleasing, unemphatic, highly educated voice. McGregor's harsh-timbred but rhythmic Scots answered him:

"They seem to be a Bohemian kind o' folk—I don't know that I rightly understand their way o' thinkin'. Not but what they can be verra decent folks. Verra pleasant to talk to and law-abiding some of 'em, too. But I find I canna' guess which way they'll jump."

Grainger laughed, "Maybe they don't always see eye to eye with the law over small details, Mac, but when it comes to what the politicians call 'the sanctity of human life' well, I'm not sure they haven't a better grasp of that than the politicians themselves. No, in a case of murder, Mac, I think you'll find the differences in your Bohemians more apparent than real. There's no limit naturally to the circumstances that can lead up to murder, but their effect on the individual who kills is always the same; he is driven to his personal limit of fear, of hate or of envy."

"What about Landru sir, or Heath?" inquired the sergeant with a grin.

Grainger finished lighting his pipe and smiled back,

"Ah, yes, Mac, you've floored me there; that's your amoral rather than your immoral murderer. But fortunately for society, such freaks of nature are comparatively rare, and however suspicious you may be of your Bohemians, you can't saddle them with a predilection for turning into Heaths!" Both men laughed, and Grainger stood up and packed the report into his briefcase.

"We may as well go straight out there," he said.

"Right, sir, I'll bring the car round," McGregor returned.

"Funny thing about the beginning of a case," Grainger remarked some twenty minutes later, as their car joined one of London's perennial traffic jams; "in a way perhaps it's the best part, a nice clean sheet, no personalities mixed up in it yet, just an interesting puzzle that's got to be solved. You know, you're the real policeman, Mac, you keep it that way to the end, don't you?"

"It's a different case, sir, my job's to do what you tell me. I'm farther from the rope than you are."

Grainger's light-lashed blue eyes regarded him through horn-rimmed spectacles.

"Very succinctly put as usual, Mac." The traffic roared and blew out carbon monoxide and the queue began to move at last. Grainger sank back into his thoughts as they wound their way through Camden Town. Even after all these years, he reflected, I feel the same about the start of a case, a compound of interest and effort; the effort of breaking into a circle of people who, however suspicious of each other, are united in their suspicion of you; the interest on the other hand of discovering the pattern of their lives and how and why murder arose out of it. The sense of effort diminished rapidly as you got your teeth into a case though...

Sergeant McGregor's thoughts as he threaded his way through the traffic were more personal. He was remembering in a ruminative, amused sort of way, what a highfalutin' fool he had considered the superior officer to whom he had been allotted ten years ago. Been up at Oxford, someone told him, taking a lot of exams in philosophy, of all unsuitable subjects for a member of the 'Force'.

He'd done his time as a 'gentstable' of course. McGregor suddenly smiled to himself, Sakes, but I'd like to ha' seen him, he thought now, squinting sideways at the superintendent's lean aristocratic figure with its scholar's stoop and clever-looking eyes. 'Course he wouldna' have had the gig-lamps then, he thought, but still! Man, though, he was a fine fellow to work for. Got right into the middle of a case while the rest were still sniffing round the edges. And methodical! Somehow he hadn't expected that; the case built up piece by piece like a jigsaw puzzle. Gave you a kick to listen to him doing it even if his lingo did take a bit of getting used to. Gave you plenty to do, too, and let you have your head. Sergeant McGregor had been won over a long time ago.

"Well, here we are." The two men got out and stood looking up at the house. "Rum old place. Must cost a small fortune to keep it running."

"As far as that goes, you're quite right," Grainger replied. "But your rum old place, my good Mac, is one of the loveliest houses in our dirty old London!"

"So long as it isna' mine," retorted the Scot dryly.

Caroline Southey let them in, her pale face worn and anxious. "Where would you like to start?" she asked.

"Oh, down below, Mrs. Southey." Paul Grainger's voice and smile were gentle and sympathetic even while the intelligent eyes behind the horn-rimmed glasses assessed the strain she was labouring under and the possible reasons for it.

"We shan't be in your way for an hour or so, but perhaps it would be convenient to have a word with you and your husband then?"

Caroline smiled back; she appreciated the superintendent's courteous phrasing of the request even while recognising that it hardly left her free to refuse.

"I'll tell my husband," she replied. "Please come up as soon as you're ready."

McGregor removed the seals on the door leading down to the basement and the two men descended. Even on this hot summer's day, the air struck chill and the smell of death lingered in the big dim rooms. Grainger walked into the dead man's living-room and stood there looking round him.

"I'll take this one first," he said. "Start in the kitchen and work round, will you, Mac." The sergeant nodded and went off.

Paul Grainger remained standing motionless in the middle of the room for some moments more; his impression of the personality which the murdered man had imprinted on his home would never again be as clear as it was now, before details had amassed to both clarify and obscure it. With deliberate leisureliness, he filled his pipe and wandered over to the bookshelves built in across one wall. He frowned as he methodically noted their contents; they told of the dead man's restless journey as an artistic Jack of all trades. It seemed he had been by turns a book-reviewer, an actor, a furniture designer, a surrealist painter—Grainger frowned and shook his head as he leafed through the puerile efforts, both Sweet's own and those of his generation. So absurd that these acolytes always ignored Jheronimus Bosch, the greatest and earliest surrealist of them all... Sweet had been interested enough in pornography to go to the trouble of acquiring some; he had been a dilettante of the *ists* and *isms* of his time.

The police officer selected a number of book reviews written by the dead man and sat down to examine them. It was apparent that Sweet's deficiencies had been spiritual rather than intellectual; his work was clever, but he showed no evidence of stature as a human being. He was caustic, merciless and denigratory, but undeniably witty. These reviews alone must have furnished him with enemies, Grainger reflected, but they would hardly have resorted to murder; unless of course the victim were sufficiently unbalanced. After all, any man might kill to protect what lies nearest to his heart... However, there seemed to be none of very recent date. He put them back and turned his attention to a small group of books he could not conceive of the dead man buying; not that they were in themselves unusual. They were leather-bound, gilt-edged classics, surely a predominantly feminine selection, belonging behind the glass doors of a Victorian lady's mahogany bookcase. He pulled one out, the leather was limp and soft, dust along the gilded edge. Yes, in faded brown copperplate, Mildred Price, and the date, 1892. For the first time he took out his notebook. Here possibly was the clue to the anomaly that was beginning to interest him; would Ivan Sweet's various activities have earned him enough to acquire his material possessions and this not uncomfortable standard of life? Well, it wasn't impossible of course, one mouth is not much to feed and Sweet had not been the type to pay income tax even if he were liable for it. He left the point open for the moment.

Sweet's desk interested him next; it was a curious affair of white wood and chromium which he had obviously made himself. Grainger unlocked the drawers and turning them out wondered why the man had troubled to lock them. In meticulous order, they contained only a variety of blank papers, all of excellent quality, graded pencils, various types of pens and rubbers, some headed writing paper and an address book of which the police officer now took possession. He sat down on the chromium flyaway stool and relit his pipe. He was personally convinced of the presence of a hidey-hole in this thirty-year-old adolescent's desk.

But where? One would expect neither originality nor finished workmanship; after a moment's consideration he removed the central drawer and measured it against the writing surface of the desk. The three-ply sliding panel revealed behind it caught at his sense of humour and he smiled as he slid it back. Inside were some photographs and a single sealed envelope. He replaced the former after an unsurprised glance and turned the envelope over in his hands—it was quite blank and plain. He slit it open with a paper-knife from the desk and took out a safe-deposit ticket. He was pleased; the pattern was growing clearer. A strangled scream made him whip round.

A pallid countenance was staring in at him through the window. At the same moment McGregor appeared in the doorway. Without turning his head Grainger said quietly:

"Go and hold on to the fellow who's standing in the area outside the window of this room, will you, Mac?"

# FOUR

THIS WAS THE MORNING OF THE THIRD DAY AFTER IVAN Sweet died; for the third time Cecil Paignton set it down in his beautiful handwriting as the first entry in his diary, but even seeing it translated thus into the manageable world of words, he could not bring himself to believe it. After staring at his diary for some time he went for a walk and walked for a long time. When he found himself creeping stealthily round the area that surrounded the basement of Magnolia House, he was afraid. He knew that he should go away, but he was as powerless to follow discretion as to believe what some remnant of reason assured him was fact. For the moment one thing only seemed of paramount importance; surely Ivan Sweet, being dead, couldn't be sitting at that desk where he had written those foul insinuations that had dogged him ever since and robbed him of his power to go on writing.

When therefore he had at last gained the window which commanded the dead man's desk, and gazing bemusedly into the dark room saw him sitting there, he screamed with very real terror and blindly tried to scramble up the area wall. Reaching the top with a supreme effort, he bumped straight into McGregor.

Grainger had climbed out of the window and now picked up the *pince-nez* that lay glittering on the damp mossed bricks of the area. He scaled the wall without difficulty and stood looking down with his gentle, intelligent eyes at the little, pale, fat man who stood in the big Scotsman's grasp, breathing heavily. He examined the bemused, round face with its child-like *retroussé* nose, the bridge deeply dented where the *pince-nez* normally clung on. He handed them back, and the little man hastily clipped them into position as if he felt a certain protection in the layer of glass through which he now looked out at the world.

"You were hoping to see Mr. Sweet?" Grainger asked quietly.

"No!"—the answer came with involuntary vehemence, and the pale blue eyes behind the glasses focused more intelligently on his questioner as he mumbled—"that is I—I—"

"You knew he had been murdered?"

"Murdered; oh. Oh, no. Er—I knew that he was dead; they said so on Saturday... he didn't come."

"Who said so?"

"Oh—er—his brother. No, it was Mr. Southey."

"You were at the party upstairs the night he was killed?"

"Yes, we all were, you know."

"All? You went with some other people?"

"No. Oh, no. I went alone."

"Can I have your name please?"

"Cecil Paignton, I'm an author..."

"Thank you. And your address?"

"Forty-six Bamford Street, N.W.1."

"I'm afraid I must ask you what your object was in coming here this morning, and why you ran away when you saw us?" Grainger continued, hardening himself with long practice to his dislike of persecuting the persecuted. The man's answer didn't altogether surprise him.

"Oh, it wasn't you!" he said at once. "I thought it was..."—confusion overtook him again—"that is... I didn't know who it was."

"And so you ran away?"

"Yes," said Paignton unhappily.

"Can you give me an account of your movements last Saturday? Perhaps you would like to see my card, we are police officers investigating the murder of Mr. Sweet."

"Yes—er—yes. I see, thank you," answered Paignton, staring helplessly at the card.

"And your movements last Saturday?" went on Grainger briskly.

"Oh, yes. Yes. I was in my room I expect… Writing," he added with more confidence.

"I see. Can anyone corroborate this?"

"Oh. Oh, yes. There's Mrs. Jarrow, she always knows what I'm doing. My landlady," he explained.

"I see. Thank you, Mr. Paignton. I needn't detain you any longer at the moment." He looked down at the flat pale face, the light glinting on the glasses making it appear blinded, impenetrable, and his glance travelled down to the small plump hands tightly encased in yellow gloves; the little man was holding his thumbs tucked in under his fingers.

"I should go home now, and get some rest," he suggested. "I expect all this has been rather a shock. Had you known Mr. Sweet long?" he added in a different tone.

The blinded head moved and the detective saw the pale eyes fixed on his own face in a strange stare.

"Yes," said Cecil Paignton, "it's been a long time."

"Eeh!" muttered the Scotsman, giving himself a little shake that was half a shudder when the writer had gone, "Yon's a queer sort o' customer!"

"Yes," replied Grainger, "he is; he's already hovering on the brink, poor unbalanced little devil, and if we have to hound him over this case it'll probably complete the process. But it's no good,

Mac, a man of Sweet's type could be dynamite to a chap like that. I've just been reading some pretty biting filth about him, or rather about some of his work. Remember that though that sort of thing seems a very slight motive to us, he might have been pressed too far. I should say there's little doubt Sweet enjoyed jabbing at him. We can't dismiss him yet."

William Southey's studio, warm under a flood of sun and languorous with the smell of oil-paint, seemed several worlds removed from the dead man's basement quarters. Paul Grainger's eyes rested involuntarily for a moment on the painter's eldest daughter posed on the model's throne and for a fraction of time his face became sealed as a memory of his wife attacked him. She had been dead now for fifteen years, killed in one of the early air-raids while he was serving overseas.

William put down his palette and brushes and turned his steady gaze on the intruder.

"Good morning, Superintendent," he said, "I wanted to ask whether you will want my daughter this morning. She and Mr. Blake"—he indicated Jonathon who sat smoking by the window—"rather wanted to go and get themselves some lunch in town."

"That will be quite in order, Mr. Southey," replied Grainger, smiling at the young couple. "If I find I have any questions for Miss Southey or Mr. Blake, they can certainly wait for another day."

"And now, Mr. Southey," he began when Jonathon and Elaine had left the room, "how long had Mr. Sweet been your tenant?"

The painter rubbed a hand over his forehead. He had seated himself on the steps of the model's throne and both men had lighted their pipes. They faced each other now through clouds of smoke, blue and swirling in the sunlight.

"It must be about nine months," William Southey said at length.

"So short a time?" asked Grainger in surprise.

"Hmm. I suppose it is," he smiled. "My wife tells me I'm a very poor judge of time."

"You knew him previously?"

"No." The monosyllable was very definite, Grainger noticed. He waited a moment but the painter didn't add anything.

"You advertised the flat, did you?"

"No. We had intended to do so." He paused a moment and the policeman would have given a lot to know what was passing in his mind, but the painter had a very stable core of reserve. An unusually honest man, who has taught himself to keep his own counsel, was Paul Grainger's mental note, but he put a query against it.

"As you will have seen," Southey went on, "this is a very large house and an old one. Fortunately I am very busy, but nevertheless we find it expensive to maintain, and I have a large family, so we eventually decided to make the house cover some of its own expenses. We first converted the attics and let them to Mrs. Moore, who was then the friend of a friend. I hadn't at that time contemplated coping with the basement, but Mrs. Moore repeatedly assured my wife and me that many people would be glad to rent it and in the end we started on it. But the work lagged rather, especially as I and my family took on a good deal of it ourselves. I think we were all beginning to feel it would never be finished when Mrs. Moore mentioned a friend who was very keen to take it and finish the conversion himself. This friend was Ivan Sweet."

"I see, thank you." Grainger paused, considering his man. At length he said, "Would I be drawing a false inference if I suggested that had it not been for these various considerations you would not have felt drawn to Mr. Sweet as a tenant?"

The observant eyes met a wary pair, and the painter smiled rather grimly.

"That would be a perfectly fair inference," he answered, "but you must understand it was no more than a quite unreasoned lack of sympathy that I felt."

"I see, thank you for your frankness, Mr. Southey."

The artist drew at his pipe but made no comment.

There was a light knock at the door and Caroline looked in.

"Would you rather I came back later?" she asked.

"Not at all, Mrs. Southey, please come in. I do hope you understand how sorry we are to disturb you in this way."

"Superintendent Grainger, we know very well that this is a job that must be done, and sooner or later it will all be over. In the meantime we are grateful to you for being so considerate."

"Thank you, Mrs. Southey; if everyone took your attitude, our work would be pleasanter. Your husband has been telling me how Mr. Sweet came to be your tenant."

He returned to the painter, "And in practice, did you find Mr. Sweet as little nuisance as you had hoped?"

There was a slight pause. He glanced at Mrs. Southey and realised that she was going to leave the answering to her husband.

"Oh yes, on the whole." Surely too easily after that tell-tale pause, thought Grainger. The painter continued, "We had perhaps been rather foolish not to take into account that, being a friend of Mrs. Moore's, he was up and down through our part of the house rather more than we had bargained for. However, it worked out pretty well…"

Grainger considered this. It was a convincing answer and contained a reason for the pause that preceded it, but the painter was a subtle man. He thought he detected a look of wifely approbation on Caroline's face.

"What were your children's reactions to him?"

He caught a quick look between husband and wife this time and felt convinced that the question had discomforted them. But Southey answered with ease:

"Perhaps you are wondering if he made unwelcome advances to my eldest daughter? As a matter of fact he did, but Elaine is a level-headed girl and too used to admiration from the opposite sex to let it turn her head. He soon gave it up when it proved so unrewarding."

"And your eldest son?"

"Richard is reading history at Cambridge and is not ordinarily here," replied Southey. Grainger didn't press him; the look of relief on Caroline's tell-tale face told him all he wanted to know. He changed his ground.

"Did it surprise you that Ivan Sweet was murdered?"

William Southey raised his eyebrows, "One is always surprised when someone is murdered," he countered.

"Quite so. But did he strike you as a man who would make enemies?" There was a fractional pause before the painter answered:

"Yes. I'm afraid he did strike me as such a man. What did you think, Caro?" he asked his wife.

"Well, yes, I'm afraid he seemed to me a naturally unkind person, Superintendent. He liked to be amusing in a way that seemed to me spiteful."

Grainger smiled despite himself. It occurred to him that these two were more likeable than he cared for in the circumstances;

he was prepared to swear that they were hiding a good deal that it would be his job to dig out. The painter in particular was deep and subtle, conceivably a dangerous man.

"Have you read any of Sweet's work?" he asked next. The involuntary reactions resulting from tangential questions seemed most likely to prove rewarding.

"No. I must confess I never had a very clear idea of what Sweet's work was. Both he and Naomi used to chatter about it but I'm afraid I didn't listen. He had one of his own pictures on the wall but he certainly wasn't a professional. I have an idea someone said he was an actor; he looked like one, perhaps he was." He turned to his wife, "You probably have a clearer idea than I, Caro. My wife is hampered by her natural courtesy, so she hears more chatter than I do."

"Well," began Caroline, "I don't know that he had any regular occupation. Naomi spoke of him as being very talented, and certainly he never seemed short of money. But I don't quite know what he did although he always gave the impression that he was very busy."

Grainger rose and held out his hand, "Well, I must thank you both for being so patient," he remarked.

"I'm afraid you must be sorely regretting that Ivan Sweet ever set foot in Magnolia House." His eyes were on them as he added this rider and he observed that both husband and wife wore a guarded expression, but that could be natural enough in the circumstances.

"I'm afraid we do feel just that, Superintendent," Caroline replied equably.

# FIVE

MRS. LION, A GOOD-NATURED SCRAWNY WOMAN WITH untidy brown hair dangling about her forward-poking neck, was the only one in Magnolia House thoroughly to enjoy the situation created by the murder.

"Me nerves'll niver be the same agin, Mr. McGregor," she told the sergeant. "There was I washin' up 'is bits o' things and 'ooverin' 'is carpets an' all the while there was 'im in that creepy ol' bafroom, the death rattle in 'is throat like as not!"

"Och, an' ye heard it, did ye?" McGregor supped his strong tea with enjoyment and hung on her every word.

"Well, no. I can't say as I akshully 'eard it," responded Mrs. Lion regretfully. "It's that there bafroom, more like one o' they old-fashioned dungeons than a decent bafroom, that is. Them walls mus' be more'n two foot thick. But I shan't niver be fergettin' of it, there was me washin' up…"

McGregor's face showed as ghoulish an interest as before, while she embarked on the tale for the third time. No one knew better than he how fatal to his purpose would be an attempt to pin her to the point. By the time he had downed his sixth cup of tea he had elucidated the following sequence: Mrs. Lion usually only reckoned to get down to the basement for an hour or so on Tuesday and Thursday afternoons. On Friday, however, Sweet had asked if she could spare half an hour to tidy up for him on Saturday morning as he had a friend coming in on Sunday (McGregor noted that Mrs. Lion assumed this to be one o' them girls of his, to the accompaniment of a significant wink). She had been a bit put out and wouldn't promise as Saturday was the day of the party. But as it turned out she had after all found herself with half an hour to spare at about twelve o'clock on Saturday. So she'd gone down, yes she had a key ('e did lock 'is door, though Mrs. Moore never), emptied his ash trays, hoovered his carpets, made his bed, done his bit of washing up (this amounted to a coffee tray for one, 'ow 'e could drink the nasty stuff and would you believe it 'e wouldn't drink tea, niver 'ad so much as a leaf of it in 'is cupboard). Yes, she answered the sergeant's query, 'e drank 'is coffee very sweet, couldn't 'ardly git the sugar orf the cup if it'd stood a bit, no, came off quite easy that morning. She had collected his rubbish together in a bin she had for the purpose and carried it straight out to the incinerator in the garden where all the rubbish for the house was burnt every day. She was a bit vague about what rubbish there had been; she'd been carrying rubbish out there all morning, what with clearing up for the party an' all. A few envelopes, she thought, no, 'e niver left letters in 'is basket, and some wrapping paper, probably a few cartons, sugar, cream, cigarettes—that sort o' thing. She had not in fact been near the bathroom which was at the end of a long passage and separated from the rest of the flat by a number of disused storage cupboards and cellars.

She didn't know whom he had been expecting that Sunday, in fact, she admitted when McGregor put the question, it might not have been a girl at all, only that he was rather a one for them.

Christine, who was perched on a high kitchen stool sucking up orange juice through a straw, suggested that perhaps it was Yolande.

"I know Dickey was awfully cross on Saturday," she continued, "and when he's cross it's usually about Yolande. You see, he wants to marry her and she likes—liked Mr. Sweet best." Mrs. Lion regarded her censoriously:

"Now what do you know about it all? You run along out into that nice sunshine." Christine looked offended but obeyed.

Mrs. Lion stole a glance at McGregor, but he gave no sign of interest in the child's chatter, and his next question reassured her as it was meant to do.

"Ye've been workin' here for a long time, maybe?"

"That I 'ave. Seven years come Christmas it'll be. Ever since Mrs. Southey come 'ere."

"Decent folk to work for?"

"Niver met better. Mrs. Southey's a real lady and always ever so friendly. Mrs. Moore now, up at the top, she's nice enough, but she don't treat you like Mrs. Southey do, she's more on 'er dignity like. Mr. Southey, 'e's a real gent, too, for all 'e spends 'is time muckin' abart in the 'ouse wiv paints and sichlike. 'Is pictures is worth ever such a lot o' money though, you wouldn't believe!"

"And this Mr. Sweet, was he a friendly sort o' chap?"

"We—ell. 'E was and 'e wasn't, if yer know wot I mean. Mostly 'e'd keep 'iself to 'iself; but if so be 'e wanted summat out o' you, then 'e was all smiles and winnin' words. Smashin' if yer likes that sort o' thing."

McGregor considered this. "Ye'd no ha' found yeself trusting the man too easy?"

"That I wouldn't. But it weren't none o' my business. Only when he started pryin' abart among Mr. Southey's things, I couldn't stand fer that, not with me the only one 'ere to keep an eye on things. And so I told 'im."

"Eh, ye did, did ye? Good for you. And did it stop him?"

Mrs. Lion looked thoughtful. "Well, 'e niver let me catch 'im at it agin."

McGregor manœuvred with care round the direct query that might have stopped the flow.

"Ye know, it's a rare thing how nosy some folks are. Why I knew a fellow once, couldna' see a desk but he wanted to pry in it. Wonderful clever he was, too; used to keep a bunch of old keys in his pocket and likely as not one of 'em would fit. Mind you, he never took anything, just nosy, that's all."

"Well 'e couldn't 'a bin nosier than Mr. Sweet. Matter o' fact 'e was tryin' ter get inter Mr. Southey's desk when I saw 'im. 'Course 'e said 'e was tryin' to put somethin' back wot Mr. Southey'd lent 'im. But 'e didn't 'ave nuffin' in 'is 'and but one o' they funny wire key things. Didn't like the look of it, I didn't."

"And quite right, too. Very suspicious behaviour I'd say. Did ye mention it to Mr. Southey, maybe?"

"Well, I didn't rightly know wot I should do. Didn't seem quite my place, if yer see wot I mean. One day when Mrs. Southey was givin' me a 'and wiv the washin' up, I took on meself to say Mr. Sweet did seem a bit snoopy-like. But Mrs. Southey she won't hear no wrong o' nobody. She just said as 'ow it takes all sorts to make a world."

McGregor decided he'd got all that was going, and not so bad at that. He looked up at the kitchen clock.

"Sakes, I been forgetting the time!" he exclaimed. "Thank ye for the tea, Mrs. Lion, ye make a guid cup o' tea. Got some body to it, that had."

Mrs. Lion displayed carious teeth in a complacent smile. "'S not wot they likes upstairs though," she remarked. "Always drinkin' that watery stuff from China. Don't taste like tea at all, I always say." McGregor was able to agree truthfully on this point and took his departure.

Naomi Moore, from her eyrie under the roofs of Magnolia House, had observed the superintendent and his sergeant arriving that morning and so was present in good order, looking, despite her years, decorative and *soignée*, when Grainger knocked on her door.

"Won't you sit down?" Naomi's brown eyes, hooded by three-cornered lids, examined him with interest behind the barrier of her smile. A man of intellectual calibre and considerable charm, he could be very attractive if he chose, she decided. She wasn't sure what she had expected of a senior police officer, but it certainly wasn't this scholarly-looking man with a voice reminiscent of—what was it? Oh yes, of course, a don. A little disconcerted, the charm of her manner intensified as she asked in her light voice with the distant ring of Irish in it.

"And what may I do for you?"

Grainger had an ingrained distrust of women who displayed a too obviously experienced charm and mentally warned himself to allow for this entirely personal prejudice before he replied:

"At this stage, Mrs. Moore, I'm afraid it's a matter of answering a lot of probably boring questions."

"I am never bored," replied Naomi with truth, "neither can I imagine that you could be boring!"

Paul Grainger smiled at her with undiminished urbanity, instinctively refusing to be drawn into personalities with this very feminine female. Nevertheless I ought to play it her way, he decided, she's curiosity incarnate, could probably be a mine of information. The effort it cost him showed no trace as he answered in a warmer tone:

"I'm afraid you flatter me, Mrs. Moore"—he brought his pipe out of his pocket and put it back again.

"Oh, do please smoke!" cried Naomi, "in fact I shall join you"—she fitted a cigarette into a holder and leant forward for him to light it.

"And now to business," she said gaily. Grainger drew on his pipe.

"Yes," he said, "now, I believe you knew Mr. Sweet better than anyone I've met yet?"

"Oh yes, Ivan and I were very old friends. I met him at a party during the war. He was an excellent person at a party, poor Ivan. Always so witty, and the most charming manners. And of course he was very gifted artistically. Are you interested in the Arts, Superintendent? I feel somehow you must be."

"Oh, yes, indeed. But unfortunately I have to spend my time conducting investigations," smiled the officer. "Mr. Sweet was an artist, was he?"

"Oh, well, not exactly. He had a very wide range of talents. He painted. You may have read some of his excellent reviews, they were so penetrating and witty. He was a dramatic critic, too, of course."

"This was during the war?"

"Yes, and afterwards, too, though I think perhaps recently he had done less literary work. Ivan was one of those people who suffered from a multiplicity of talents, you know; I used to suggest to him sometimes that he might find it more rewarding to concentrate on *one* of his gifts, but," she shrugged and smiled tolerantly, "he wouldn't listen."

"He was not called upon for armed service or civil defence work during the war?"

Naomi regarded him with great seriousness.

"I feel sure I can be frank with you, Superintendent," she said solemnly, "especially as poor Ivan is now dead?"

"Of course." Grainger waited, puffing quietly at his pipe. After giving him another searching look, she continued, "I happen to know that Ivan applied for exemption as a conscientious objector." She hesitated a moment.

"His appeal was not granted." There was censure in her tone, but not for Ivan Sweet.

"He spent some time in prison, then?" Grainger remarked, hoping he had hit the right conversational note.

"Well, no. Actually he didn't."

"I see," he paused. "Then I suppose he had to move around a good deal, then?"

"Oh yes, poor Ivan, he was very much here today and gone tomorrow. I was never surprised when he vanished for a few months."

Grainger reflected grimly but silently that at that period nobody was very surprised when people vanished out of this life altogether. How quite extraordinarily ego-centric some of these artistic parasites could be, in such contrast to the productive artists whose poetry of words or form came back, all too often without the artist, from the mud of Flanders or the bitterly contested air of Britain, or whose hard-felt convictions drove them to ambulance units under enemy fire.

"He must have suffered some financial embarrassment, I imagine?" he asked next.

"If he did, he never mentioned it. In fact it was rather an odd thing about Ivan, he never did mention money. Most unusual, really."

"Yes indeed," responded Grainger, for the first time with genuine amusement. Sweet's financial affairs were obviously due for an early and exhaustive check.

"Was it coincidence that you found yourself living in the same house this last few months?"

"Oh no, not at all. It was my suggestion," replied Naomi at once, unconsciously corroborating the Southeys. "Ivan was looking for somewhere to live, and he was very keen about the flat when I mentioned it. And, of course, he was so clever at converting things and decorations and so on. I was rather pleased with myself for bringing it about." She smiled complacently.

"The Southeys liked him did they?"

"Well, yes, I think so. Perhaps Ivan felt sometimes that they weren't as sociable with him as he might have liked. But on the whole it was a very satisfactory arrangement."

"I'm sure you will understand, Mrs. Moore," Grainger leant forward confidentially, "that we are bound to be very interested in any enemies Mr. Sweet may have felt he had. As a close friend of his, I'm hoping you may be able to help us here."

Naomi got up and fetched herself another cigarette.

"Well, of course," she remarked when she was seated again, "that's a very difficult question to answer, isn't it, Superintendent? I shouldn't really like to feel that I might have directed your suspicions against anyone."

Grainger embarked on one of his set pieces.

"In every investigation we undertake, Mrs. Moore, a great deal of irrelevant matter turns up; you know the sort of thing, bad feeling about various incidents, petty or otherwise, spite and jealousy. You know as well as I do that this is just the stuff of everyday life, and in the ordinary way, the less said about it the better. But when a murder has been committed, unfortunately for everyone involved, it has to be sifted through. But I can promise you that we exercise absolute discretion over everything that doesn't directly concern our case."

"Well, if I can really feel that," she flashed a smile at him, "and I'm sure I can take your word for it, I will tell you anything I can." She smoked thoughtfully in silence for a few moments, and Grainger thought, now that he saw her without the camouflage of her volubility, that she might be more formidable than she appeared at first sight.

"Of course, there's no denying," the musical Irish voice started again, "that Ivan did sometimes arouse ill feeling. He had a very biting sense of humour which upset some people. There was an actor who committed suicide and people did say... well, you won't want old history. Little Cecil Paignton couldn't bear him of course, but he would be quite incapable of killing anyone, although he is a bit peculiar in his own way. But then so are lots of us, aren't we, Superintendent?" She laughed. She had a musical laugh and knew it, thought Grainger.

"Oh, yes, you could rule out poor little Cecil, a pathetically ineffective person I'm afraid, poor little man." Some curious flavour in her remark caught at Grainger's attention, but he couldn't analyse it.

"Of course," she went on, "Ivan was a most attractive young man; women used to fall for him very heavily; foolish of them to let it be so obvious, but we women are foolish where men are concerned, aren't we?" Grainger forced himself to return her smile of complicity, "And there's no denying that that sort of thing does arouse some very strong feelings, is there?" she continued.

Grainger assented. "You haven't any particular names in mind?" he asked invitingly.

"Well, I think that most of those I had in mind were rather long ago to be important now... you know how it was during the war, so many young girls with their husbands away... Of course, some people do have long memories... But I feel recent history is more useful for you. I did notice that that rather charming child Yolande Meade who lives with her father near by had become very much attached to him. Her father was greatly upset, I believe, he's an old-fashioned type and quite out of sympathy with Ivan." She frowned thoughtfully: "Mrs. Jonas at the cottage next door was attracted, but—I don't really think it likely that Ivan would have given her Edouard any cause for jealousy, although it's true he did spend a surprising amount of time over there." She laughed, "I must confess I never could understand why! Of course," she added suddenly, "there's Ivan's brother." Her eyes narrowed. "I suppose if Ivan had anything to leave, Pat Sweet could have been involved."

"Do you think he might have had anything to leave?" asked Grainger rather sharply. Naomi looked up at him, startled.

"I don't know," she answered.

But he wasn't quite sure if he believed her.

# SIX

WHILE GRAINGER AND MCGREGOR WORKED THROUGH Magnolia House, listening, looking, sifting impression and fact, Jonathon and Elaine walked across the hot grass in Hyde Park, the warm breeze rustling among the leaves of the dappled plane trees and blowing in their hair. The passers-by, expanding in the summer heat, smiled to see them pass, so alight with love and youth that they made amends for all the muddle and waste, the dreariness and misshapenness of the rest of humanity.

But the horror that kept gruesome company with Elaine through the merciless emptiness of night would not be exorcised for long. As Jonathon drove her out of the park in search of lunch she felt the shivers of apprehension running through her again.

"What is it, darling?"

"Oh. I—I suppose I was thinking of poor Mother and Father. While we've been enjoying ourselves, they're being grilled by the police."

Jonathon's face sobered.

"It's horrible," he agreed. "Of all the swinish luck, that chap getting himself killed in your house. The night we met, too! I could murder him myself if he weren't dead already." He frowned as he negotiated the little car through the teeming traffic.

"What sort of fellow was he? Nobody's said much, but I got the impression he might have been rather a thorn in the flesh."

"That's just the trouble. He was. We took as little notice of
him as possible, but it was difficult to ignore him as much as we'd
have liked. He had a way of cropping up in the conversation, and
then he was somehow one of those people you can't forget are in
the house. Even when I couldn't see or hear him I could feel him
being down there. I know I used to get a quite ridiculous sense of
relief when I saw him go out, and I often thought it was the same
for the others, too, although nobody ever mentioned it except
Richard who spent most of this vac. going into rages about him."

Jonathon gave her a startled glance, "What had he done to
upset Dick then?"

"Plenty. Though I suppose it wasn't strictly Sweet's fault. Do
you remember a pretty, fair girl who was at the party with her
father? He's the nice old man who was managing the gramophone—incidentally he was another one who felt absolutely
murderous about Ivan Sweet..." She stopped, appalled by what
she had said.

"Darling, that's just a figure of speech, and a common one at
that. Don't let that sort of detail worry you."

She smiled at him gratefully, "You are a comforting person,
Jon. Well, Richard and Yolande spent most of his last vac. going
about together and when he went back to Cambridge, he was very
full of it all and wrote to her every day," she smiled. "I believe he
even wrote her poems! Anyway after a week or two we began
getting anxious letters from him. Apparently she had stopped
writing. But she wasn't ill; she wasn't writing to Dick because she
was spending all her spare time with Ivan Sweet. Incidentally, he
had been rather occupied up to that time by making advances to
me—all right, darling, don't explode, that's what Gideon used to
do and it was so ridiculous because I loathed the man..."

"Who's Gideon?"

"Darling, I introduced you to him at the party."

"You mean that melancholy weed with long hair who was hanging about and getting under our feet?"

Elaine smiled ruefully, "Poor Gideon," she said, "yes, that would be he."

"Well, I won't interrupt you now," remarked Jonathon grimly, "we'll deal with Gideon later. Go on."

"You make it jolly difficult to go on," retorted the girl with spirit. "But the end of the story's probably pretty clear by now. Yolande fell for Sweet hook, line and sinker, and we were left with the beastly job of wondering what to tell poor Richard. And of course you can imagine what he's been like ever since and what he feels, I should say felt, about Sweet... and now he's dead and..." Her voice tailed away and Jonathon realised suddenly that despite the warmth of the day she was shivering. He drove on in the uneasy silence, his young face very serious. They were approaching the embankment now, and the sun, with a perfect sense of timing, had disappeared behind a cloud, leaving the streets mean and dusty-looking.

"Well, of course, it's an abominable position," he said at last, "but, after all, trying to look at it dispassionately, this sort of thing is happening every day, getting pipped on a girl I mean, and however ghastly it is for everyone, people don't up and commit murder on account of it, do they?"

"I suppose they do sometimes," said Elaine miserably.

"Maybe, but not Dick. After all it's not as though Sweet was knocked down in a fit of temper, or something like that that one could just conceivably imagine Dick doing. This must have been cold-blooded, premeditated murder; the chap was in his bath with the water over his head, and there weren't any injuries that I could see. His sponge had partially blocked the overflow—he must have been lying there keeping the bath warm with the hot tap, that was why it dripped over on to the floor and trickled out into the passage. Why he should have drowned in it we shan't know until the inquest, though I dare say somebody knows by now or they wouldn't be calling it murder. My guess is someone poisoned him before he got into his bath. Now, however much Dick loathed the chap, you can't see him planning a cold-blooded murder, can you?"

Elaine was silent for a moment. Finally she said, "No, I can't. No, Jon you're absolutely right. It was just muddled thinking, wasn't it?" There was a note of appeal in her voice and Jonathon realised with something like alarm that she wasn't quite convinced. Oh God, he thought, but he said calmly enough:

"That's the way I see it."

"And you're absolutely right." There was a short silence and then she asked:

"Where are we going for lunch?"

"To the Blue Macaw, it's rather jolly, candlelight and that sort of thing."

"And with whom have you dined there by candlelight?" asked Elaine lightly as they entered a charming bow-windowed house facing the river.

"Oh… duty dinner."

"Hmm. Do aunts appreciate candlelight?"

"I didn't say she was an aunt."

"So it was a she?"

"If you want to know," Jonathon was on his dignity, "I got myself let in for taking a friend's sister out."

"Like me. I'm Dick's sister."

"She could scarcely have been more *un*like you. Had you seen her you would have been sorry for me."

"So you thought she might look better by candlelight?"

"She would have been hideous by any light," replied the young man uncompromisingly. He turned to her with the air of one who has settled the matter and was scandalised to find her struggling with laughter.

"You little minx!" he exclaimed, but he was relieved, the catechism had seemed out of character.

It was some time later, when they had finished eating and were sipping their coffee, that Elaine said, a little hesitatingly, "Jon?"

"What is it, love?"

"Do my mother and father seem to you as if... as if they were under a strain?" Jonathon's reddish brows drew together as he considered the question.

"Well, of course, I haven't met them under normal conditions. With a murder in the house it would seem unnatural to me if they weren't a little strained."

"Yes, of course," answered Elaine, "you never knew them as they were before..."

Jonathon asked, "You feel a bit worried about them?"

Elaine frowned as she stared down at the polished table, tracing patterns on the shining surface with her warm finger.

"I wouldn't tell anyone but you, Jon, but you are so comforting and so—balanced. You can see it from outside more than I can. I've got the most horrid nightmare feeling that Daddy hasn't been quite the same for—oh it must be some seven months. I remember one particular evening; Mummy was out and it was term time so Dick wasn't there, and I'd been out and had come in earlier than I'd expected. Well, you can just see the door of Daddy's studio when you're a little way up the stairs, and when I reached there that night, it was dark, November, I think it was. There was the light of Daddy's door opening, and I was just going to call up to him, when I saw that it was Ivan Sweet who was coming out. I didn't want to meet him, so I went quickly downstairs and into the cloak-room. When he'd gone through the door into the basement with those beastly, stealthy steps of his, I went up to Daddy.

"Ivan hadn't shut the studio door properly and I pushed it open and went in. Daddy was sitting at that untidy old desk by the window, we always tease him about it and say he keeps his past in there, for it's the only thing he ever locks. He was sitting there with his head in his hands and he looked—oh as if something terrible had happened. I stood there not knowing what to do, I thought if I went away again he might hear me and that would be worse. In the end I crept back to the door and stood just outside and called 'Hallo, Daddy, I'm early', and came in again after a minute. He got up and he was trying to look like his usual self, but he—he couldn't! I knew then that I was right, something terrible had happened. I didn't know what to do. Daddy never likes to be interfered with when things go wrong, so I said 'It's a beastly foggy night outside, I'd like a drink. Shall I pour you one, too?' And he said in an awful strangled sort of voice, 'Yes thank you, Elaine, I'd like one.' I poured him a stiff whisky and he took it without a word and drank it straight down. I couldn't help noticing that his hand was shaking. After a while he said, 'I think I'll turn in, I feel a bit under the weather tonight. Will you sit up for your mother and tell her that I've gone to bed?' After he'd gone I sat there sort of shivering with fright, you know how one does. And the more I thought about it, the more certain I felt that Sweet had something to do with the terrible thing, whatever it was."

Shivers were running down Jonathon's spine as he said, "You're quite right, Elaine, you mustn't repeat that story to anyone, not even your own family." Seeing her terrified look, he went on quickly, "Sweetheart, I'm convinced your father would never kill a man, but in the circumstances that's a very damaging story and the less people who know about it the better." His eyes rested on her compassionately, "Poor darling, no wonder you wanted to tell someone." She looked at him, not trusting herself to speak.

"I'll get the bill and we'll get out of here," he went on. "I think we'll take a little run into the country. O.K.?"

"How was he next day?" he asked when they were in the car and going south out of London.

"He did get flu oddly enough," Elaine answered, "though as a rule he never catches it. I wondered if it could have been the shock of—whatever it was?"

Jonathon nodded. "Might well have been," he agreed. "Shock lowers the defences and we get all sorts of things when that happens."

"When he was up again, he was very much his usual self, but I couldn't help feeling every now and then, that he was *being* himself with an effort."

"Hmm... You spoke in the beginning as though you were worried about your mother as well?"

"Well, yes, though I'm not very sure. I think she put Daddy's oddness at that time down to flu, but the last couple of months or so I've thought she seemed different, too. But I don't know, it may all be me."

"Mmm. Well, sooner or later they'll turn up the murderer and we can forget all these horrid fancies for good and all. Let's hope it's sooner."

"Oh, I hope so! You know every sort of thing seems to have been disturbing the last few months; poor Dick and Yolande, and even Naomi, you know the woman who lives in the top flat. She had two beastly experiences only a week or so ago."

"Oh, what happened to her?"

"Well, the first was in the middle of the night; she woke up out of a dream that she was being gassed to discover that it was true. She's got one of those gas cooking-rings in her bedroom and always makes herself a nightcap before she goes to sleep. Well that night I suppose it must have got blown out or something, and she thought it was off and went to sleep. When she woke up, she just managed to stagger out on to the landing. Fortunately I heard her. She was horribly sick and dizzy, poor soul, but she wasn't too bad the next day except for a shocking headache."

"Poor woman, what a ghastly thing to happen. She was lucky though to wake up when she did."

"I know. And as if that wasn't enough, a week later she fell down the flight of stairs leading up to her flat. It's a steep flight and it's amazing she didn't do herself any serious damage, because she's not young."

"What a chapter of accidents! It's funny how they always seem to run together. But now we're going to forget all about them and think about us!"

Which they did, and no jarring note was struck until they drew up outside Magnolia House again. Then Jonathon said, "I know, I'll go home and change and we'll go dancing. The perfect end to a perfect day!" Elaine was delighted, but suddenly her face clouded.

"Oh, but I can't!" she said. She glanced at her watch, "I'm late already, oh dear."

"Late for what?"

"For Gideon. I promised to go to the theatre with him tonight. Oh damn!"

Jonathon's disappointment and jealousy fanned his quick temper into an alarming rage.

"You can't go out with that fellow!" he almost shouted.

"Darling!" pleaded Elaine, "it's the last thing I want to do, I'd love to come dancing…"

"Well come on then."

"Darling I can't. I promised him weeks ago."

"If you love me you can't go with that man tonight!" said Jonathon furiously.

Elaine's temper suddenly rose to meet his.

"You're being totally unreasonable. I must go and that's the end of it. Moreover I must go now. I trust you'll have come to your senses by tomorrow."

"You won't be seeing me tomorrow!" Jonathon threw the car into gear and drove furiously down the hill.

Elaine stood alone watching him, filled with such despair as she had never known. It couldn't, oh, it couldn't end like this!

# SEVEN

WHILE JONATHON AND ELAINE WERE ANXIOUSLY TALKING at the Blue Macaw, the superintendent and his sergeant were discussing the case over bread and cheese and beer in a pub near Magnolia House.

Grainger listened with amusement to McGregor's account of his tea-drinking orgy with Mrs. Lion. He nodded when the sergeant came to the charwoman's discovery of Sweet tampering with the painter's desk.

"Yes," he answered, "I was expecting something like that." He produced the envelope containing the safe-deposit ticket.

"I found these behind what the fellow imagined to be a secret panel in that home-made desk of his. I want you to run down and get the stuff out this afternoon, Mac. Whatever he kept in there will probably crack this case wide open."

The sergeant took the ticket with alacrity and tucked it into an inner pocket. Grainger finished his beer and began to fill his pipe.

"It's a pity, from our point of view," he remarked, "that the charwoman washed up his breakfast and tipped his rubbish on to that incinerator of theirs. The analyst's report shows a heavy overdose of sodium amytal."

"Does it? Mm, poisoned first and drowned afterwards. Aye, that was the way you said t'wad be," nodded the Scot.

"The point the child made about her elder brother fits in with his parents' reticence about him. I don't see this murderer as a nineteen-year-old boy but these things can happen as we'd do well to remember. I haven't seen him yet. Incidentally, Mrs. Lion seems very devoted to the family, doesn't she?"

"That's a fact. But I doubt she's holding anything back."

"Good. I wondered." Grainger gave the sergeant a résumé of his own findings. "It begins to make a pattern with yours, doesn't it?" he finished. "It looks as though we may have plenty of candidates though. We shall need the usual financial inquiries of course; if you've time, get the preliminaries sorted out. I'll see Sweet's bank manager as soon as I can. Nothing like the passage of money to tell a story at this stage!"

He got up. "See you later, Mac."

Paul Grainger walked out into the strong sunlight, blinking as it struck his glasses. The heat seemed to be bouncing off the pavement in waves and the brilliant light struck an answering sparkle from the shining fragments embedded in the big square stones. It was very quiet. He walked slowly downhill towards Magnolia House, the sound of his footsteps echoing in his own ears. He felt rocked by the heat from his normal intellectual detachment to something more physical, but still detached. Almost more so. A park lay beyond tall railings on his right; he stopped and stared through them for an idle moment, his eyes resting on the grateful green, the sun's warm clasp on his shoulder. His eyes wandered without effort of thought over the grass, the trees, the flower beds and he was reminded suddenly of the satisfactions of gardening. It must be years since I had a spade or a trowel in my hand, he thought. I mustn't get into a rut, he decided, it's a danger when one lives alone; I don't know though, probably a danger anyway time you get to my age. I suppose I shall be thirty-nine next birthday. His mind skipped back through the years until he called it back to heel like a well-disciplined dog.

Ah well, he thought, now for interviewing a love-sick youth, nineteen and still at Cambridge! He shook his head and turned into the main road.

Richard had a pleasant but quite fantastically untidy room. He was a lean dark boy, not as good-looking perhaps as the rest of the family, but with that energy of personality that can be more attractive than good looks.

Grainger offered him a cigarette. "Your father tells me you are reading history," he remarked conversationally.

"Yes."

"A good subject. I considered it myself once. What's your college?"

"Trinity; were you up there?"

"No, I was at the other place." They both smiled at the well-worn joke. How odd to think I might have had a boy almost as old as this, Paul Grainger was thinking; his wife had been pregnant when she was killed. Aloud he said, "Well, this is pleasant but I suppose we should get down to business. What can you tell me about the man Ivan Sweet?"

"He was a swine," replied Richard simply.

"So I rather gathered. People who get themselves murdered quite frequently are. What was particularly objectionable about him?"

"Oh... he was just a thoroughly nasty piece of work. Born like it I suppose, like that ghastly child next door. She pushed my sister out of a tree a few years back. Chris was only four at the time and Theresa was seven. It was damn lucky it didn't break her neck. I saw her do it, out of pure spite. I gave her a beating—caused a hell of a rumpus but it stopped her coming over here."

"Mm, nasty. And what about Sweet, did you give him a beating, too?"

"Wish I had. Too late now."

"Quite so. I take it you didn't murder him?"

"Of course not. Wouldn't have solved anything. I was out all day Saturday anyway." He looked reflectively at Grainger, "That's probably the sort of thing you want to know, isn't it?"

"Please."

Richard considered. "I was like a bear with a sore head that day, I'm afraid," he said. "Makes it difficult to remember times and things. I have an idea I behaved rather badly and cleared off after breakfast."

"Where did you clear off to?"

"Oh, I mooched about on the heath; it was a lovely day though I wasn't in the mood to appreciate it. The place was thick with courting couples enjoying themselves." His face had darkened again.

"You didn't meet anyone who might remember having seen you?"

"Can't remember. Probably wouldn't have taken any notice if I did. I wasn't feeling sociable."

"Well, let your memory have a go at it and let me know if anything comes up. What about lunch? Did you come back?"

"No, I had a sandwich and a beer in a pub; it was the Hand in Hand."

"And after that?"

"I went to the Metropole. They had on a revival of *The Blue Angel*."

"And then?"

"Oh, I did meet someone then. Old Matty, we were at school together. He's got a room in Hampstead, he asked me to go back with him and brew a pot of tea, so I went and we jawed a bit."

"And after that?"

"Oh, I walked back and dropped in on a friend who lives near here, and then came on home; I was late by then and had to rush around getting dressed for Elaine's party."

"Good. If you could just give me the addresses of your two friends I needn't bother you any more."

Grainger walked slowly up the path to the front door of Magnolia Cottage. Behind it a woman's voice could be heard, shrilly haranguing someone who answered, when he had a chance, in a lower tone. Grainger rang the bell but the noise within continued unabated. He waited a moment before trying the knocker and was suddenly aware of being watched. He made no movement but under the useful cover of his glasses his eyes raked the bushes and discerned a pale blue eye gleaming under a bony forehead. An isolated spy session, he wondered, treating the unresponsive door to a decisive rap, or an established habit perhaps? The voices within had ceased abruptly and there was the faint but unmistakable sound of feet taking to stairs. Aerial reconnaissance now, thought the detective, and sure enough a bedroom curtain moved and a face appeared pallidly behind the dark pane.

The door was opened at last by a plain woman with clever eyes. Her lips drew back in an unappetising smile and she said with an attempt at affability, "It's Superintendent Grainger, isn't it?"

He looked faintly surprised perhaps, for she went on, "Oh, I saw you the other night when poor Ivan Sweet got himself murdered in that house. Do come in." She stood aside to let him pass and ushered him into a sitting-room, sprouting with school photographs in which he noticed the Jonas family, all rather regrettably perpetuated.

"Do sit down, Superintendent, and tell me how I can help you. Poor Ivan Sweet was always such a welcome visitor here and I should be only too glad to do anything I can to help you find his murderer—or murderess," she added. Paul Grainger wondered whether this was feminine spite or mere pedantry.

"Thank you, Mrs. Jonas. You are very strategically placed here near the scene of the crime."

Barbara Jonas ignored the double implication of this remark, and replied brightly, "Oh, indeed we are. Really we cannot help but see the comings and goings at Magnolia House. In fact they are a very great disturbance to us; when we came here eight years ago the house was empty, but now—the Southeys are such a large family"—she made it sound indecent—"and so noisy. And now that they take in lodgers, of course, it's even worse, though I must admit that I did have a soft spot for Ivan. He had charming manners, quite charming."

"Had you known Mr. Sweet long?" asked Grainger.

"Before he came to that house you mean? Poor fellow, how tragic that he should ever have come there!…"

"Is it your opinion that his murder is connected with his residence at Magnolia House then?" inquired Grainger mildly. Mrs. Jonas's eyes opened wide.

"Oh, but surely! Don't you think so, Superintendent?"

"As a police officer I have to be wary of hasty conclusions, but I should be interested to hear your arguments."

Mrs. Jonas regarded him with calculating eyes, "Well, Superintendent, living as close as we do and seeing a good deal of Ivan, it was impossible not to realise that the whole family disliked the poor boy very much."

"Even so, it is unusual surely to murder an unwelcome tenant?"

"Yes," conceded the woman unwillingly, "but I'm sure there was more to it than that. That boy of theirs, for instance, he has a savage and uncontrollable temper; we should know for he used to bully our little girl. He was so dangerous that we had to forbid her to play in their garden. And only the other night, I—I was doing a bit of watering, after the heat of the sun, you know, and I actually heard him threatening Ivan."

"Do you happen to remember the actual phrase?"

"Oh yes, certainly. Knowing his murderous temper it made my blood run cold. He said, 'If you don't leave her alone, Sweet, I'll break your bloody neck for you.'"

"What night would this have been?"

"Friday. The night before the murder."

"Who was the woman to whom young Southey was referring? Do you know?"

"It must have been Yolande Meade. An insipid little blonde who lives near here with a doting father. The sort of silly girl boys of that age always behave stupidly about. She's trying to be an actress, but she hasn't the intelligence to get very far in that line. Bone from the neck up, nothing to recommend her but a sickly, chocolate box simper, but the fools fall for it."

The door had opened and Edouard's pretty narrow-featured face was peering round it.

"Oh come, dear," he remarked, "she may not have your brains but she's a pretty little thing. Good afternoon, Superintendent," he added, smiling at Grainger in an ingratiating way. "Would it be in order if I come in, or are you taking us one at a time, like boys in the headmaster's study?" He made a sound unpleasantly like a giggle.

"Of course you can come in, Edouard, if you don't make a fool of yourself," replied his wife before Grainger had a chance to speak. "As we live so near That House the superintendent thought we might have noticed something that would help him with his case. I've just been telling him about that murderous boy, Richard Southey..."

"I think your wife has not entirely understood my position," Grainger interpolated firmly; "at this stage of an investigation we question all the dead man's associates who may have had access to him at the time of the crime. I understand that Mr. Sweet was a friend of yours?"

"Oh—er, yes." Edouard looked frightened. "He—he was by way of being a friend of Barbara's." His wife gave him a look which still further reduced his morale.

"That was Theresa at the window just now, go and fetch her in, Edouard," she ordered.

Behind his spectacles Paul Grainger blinked. What a household! Nevertheless it was always possible that some of this woman's verbal poison had a foundation in fact.

"Did you notice any person other than those normally belonging to the household visiting Magnolia House on Saturday?"

"Oh, no, just the family, in and out, in and out all the time, and those guttersnipes shrieking round the garden."

"You definitely noticed no other people coming or going, or loitering near the house that day?" persisted Grainger.

"There was some young fool hanging about during the morning. I thought at the time he was after Elaine Southey—what these young men see in her I can't think, I suppose with that house they get the impression her father has a lot of money..."

"You could not identify this young man?" interrupted Grainger.

"Oh I found out that night who he was. It was Ivan's brother."

"Mr. Patrick Sweet?"

She nodded.

"Did you see him enter the house?"

Mrs. Jonas considered. "No, when I saw him he was looking down at the area windows of his brother's flat—I think it's disgusting to charge anyone for living in a beastly dank basement like that, don't you?"

"It seems unlikely that there was any compulsion on Mr. Sweet to make him take that particular flat," Grainger responded dryly. "At what time of the morning did you notice the brother?"

"Let me see, I was cleaning my windows, it would have been about eleven, I suppose."

"And you saw no one else?"

"Only old Meade."

"Oh? At what time?"

"Oh," Mrs. Jonas sounded impatient. "Earlier, say half-past ten."

"Thank you. And now for your own movements that day?"

"Saturday, you mean. Why you should be interested in my movements I can't conceive, but I suppose you can't help all your petty rules and regulations. Well then, I was working in the house all the morning and my husband and Theresa were in the garden. They were supposed to be gardening, but they didn't get much done. However, that's where they were. In the afternoon I had a rest and Edouard took Theresa for a walk on the heath."

"Thank you, Mrs. Jonas. If I can just confirm that with your husband and daughter I can get on my way."

However, if Edouard and Theresa wanted to add anything they didn't achieve the necessary verbal space and finally Grainger left.

# EIGHT

I T WAS ONLY TEN MINUTES' WALK TO HENRY MEADE'S COTTAGE. Paul Grainger glanced up at it with appreciation; it was built in that particularly appealing late Georgian style that allows one wing to deviate from absolute severity into a pleasing curve. It pleases the eye rather as a voluptuous woman does when she wears a well-tailored suit, he thought, and smiled at the whimsical analogy. He swung open the well-oiled gate and walked up a pathway of old herringboned brick, admiring the passionately flowering roses and the smooth green turf. Fresh from the discordant chaos of the Jonas home these proofs of care and discipline were soothing.

The tall old man who opened the door was in keeping with his setting; in the cool book-lined room where his host courteously installed him in a comfortable wing chair, Grainger noted on the shelves the calf-bound volumes of Wordsworth and Tennyson that all else had predicated.

"I believe it's nearly tea-time," remarked Meade, glancing at the discreet grandfather clock that ticked solemnly from its shadowy corner; "am I permitted to ask you to join me?"

"Some tea would be most welcome," the detective responded with truth.

"If you'll forgive me for a moment, I'll just tell my housekeeper."

Left alone, Paul Grainger relaxed with a sigh of satisfaction; what a great deal there was to be said for this courteous and orderly generation, he thought. The room with its ascetic aestheticism pleased him. It was a room, he thought, to read in and his mind wandered to the pretty actress daughter. Had the unspoken discipline of such a room perhaps played its part in driving her to such a fellow as Sweet? What traps love sets for itself, he thought; her father's love protecting her with what he conceived to be fitting, and her love driving her to all that was farthest from it.

"And how can I help you, Superintendent?" asked Henry Meade when he returned.

"As you know, sir, I am investigating the murder of Mr. Sweet, at Magnolia House, the day before yesterday. I believe that you and your daughter were present at Miss Southey's party on that night, and that you were both acquainted with the dead man?"

"Yes. Both those facts are quite correct."

"I would like you to tell me how well you knew Mr. Sweet, sir."

"Quite so." Meade regarded the detective thoughtfully. "Well, Superintendent, possibly you realise that your question is not an easy one for me to answer. But if I may say so, I have the greatest confidence in our police force, and in addition I have always considered the truth to be the only tenable policy, so I shall do my best to be frank with you, although you will soon realise that this is somewhat distasteful to me in that it involves my daughter Yolande, whom you will no doubt wish to question later."

"Thank you, sir. May I say I appreciate your position."

"You ask me how well we knew Ivan Sweet. I will prelude that by remarking that had the choice been mine, we would not have known him at all. My daughter is seventeen, as you doubtless know a most impressionable and rather restless age. She is also not without attraction. Young men of Mr. Sweet's type—I can only hope there are not many such—are the very last influence

I would have chosen for her. You can therefore well imagine my feelings when I found that she was becoming infatuated with this very undesirable young man, and that, moreover, he was taking advantage of this to undermine my influence over her. I believe he had promised to give her some help in her career. She wants to be an actress, you know. I will not try to conceal from you that my first reaction to the news of his death was one of heartfelt relief. This may sound a most improper reaction to the death of a fellow creature, but I don't know whether you have any daughters…"

"Unhappily, no."

"Well, they are a great pleasure and a great anxiety, Superintendent. The more so possibly in my case since Yolande's mother died in giving birth to her and she sorely lacks a woman's guidance."

A light knock sounded on the door and an elderly woman brought in the tea. The trolley looked singularly inviting with its fine porcelain and Georgian silver. Grainger found himself wishing that this was the social occasion it seemed, and not the interview that was required. But he went on, "I feel sure you understand, Mr. Meade, that in the circumstances I have to ask for your movements, with verification where possible, throughout last Saturday."

"Of course." The old man's face showed no sign of what he might be feeling as he took out a pocket diary and put on his spectacles.

"Saturday, yes." He had found the page. "Yolande was unwell that morning, I had her breakfast taken up to her and sat over mine with a book. Afterwards I took a stroll round my garden and did the watering before the sun got too hot. I expect my housekeeper can bear me out so far. Then I went up to see Yolande, but she was asleep, so I took my hat and stick and walked over to Hampstead for a late coffee. I was back at one-thirty for lunch, and took a short nap in my chair afterwards. When I awoke it wanted half an hour or so to tea and I decided to treat one or two of my roses for greenfly. As so often happens in the garden, I forgot the time and my housekeeper finally called me in. Yolande had come down meanwhile and we had tea together. Afterwards we talked for a while and young Richard Southey dropped in. By the time he went we needed to make haste to be ready for Elaine's party. Is that what you want, Superintendent?"

"An admirably clear account, thank you, sir. There's just one small point, did you pass Magnolia House on your way to Hampstead?" Henry Meade's old blue eyes met Grainger's for a moment and he gave a small smile.

"As you know, it is in the opposite direction; but I should have mentioned that I went down that way first. I had considered calling in, but decided that Mrs. Southey would be very busy with her party preparations, so I went to Hampstead instead."

"Thank you, Mr. Meade, I'm glad to have that point cleared up."

Experienced police officer though he was, Grainger couldn't help but be a little embarrassed to find that he had arrived at Pat Sweet's one-room flat at the baby's feeding-time. There was a sort of cubby-hole on the landing and he suggested to the young husband that he be questioned there. Pat, however, refused, almost as if he enjoyed the other's discomfiture and this blatant exhibition of the poverty in which his family lived. For lack of a chair that wasn't covered with clothes and nappies, Grainger settled himself on the end of the bed with his back to the young mother. The baby sucked noisily and he frowned uncomfortably as he got out his notebook.

"I will endeavour not to keep you long," he remarked. "First, can you tell me when you last saw your brother alive?"

"Heaven knows! I never saw him if I could help it."

"You hadn't seen him recently then?"

"Don't think so."

"Not on the morning of the murder for instance?"

"Lord no! Once a day was enough to see Ivan. I knew I'd see him that night."

"Were you in the vicinity of Magnolia House that morning?"

"What are you getting at?" The man was suddenly aggressive. "Does somebody say I was?"

"I'm afraid I must ask you to answer my question, Mr. Sweet."

"Why the devil should I?"

"You can refuse to answer if you prefer; but I would of course put my own interpretation on your refusal."

"Bloody Gestapo! Why the devil do you have to come interfering with me? I didn't choose Ivan for a brother... why do you have to tangle me up in his affairs?"

"I'm making no such attempt, Mr. Sweet. You are inevitably concerned. Your brother has been murdered and you appear to be his only relative; do you know of any others?"

"Ivan and I were orphans and bastards."

"It seems probable then that you will be his heir. We have found no will."

"You won't find he had anything to leave. I know Ivan always saw to it that he lived soft, he wasn't such a mug as me, he kept out of the forces, but he was no fonder of work than I am. You'll probably find he lived on credit—and women."

"I'm afraid I still require to know whether you were in the vicinity of Magnolia House on Saturday morning."

"I may have been," answered Pat indifferently. "I was loafing about here and there. You could put that down as my occupation if you like, loafing—with artistic pretensions, don't forget those, they're my claim to distinction."

Grainger ignored this. He continued:

"I gather you were not attached to your brother?"

"I thought he was loathsome."

"But you didn't kill him?"

"No. I'm congenitally lazy, ask my wife. Besides it would have been a 'good work' and I'm averse to good works."

"What did you do on Saturday afternoon?"

"I went to the Zoo."

His small daughter gave an outraged cry, "Oh, Daddy, why didn't you take me with you?" and his wife chimed in, "Yes, if you were going, you might have taken her, Pat. And why ever did you go on a Saturday when it's cheaper on Monday?"

"Oh, hell, why, why, why! You drive me crazy. If you really want to know I wanted to make some sketches."

"Perhaps you can help me in another direction, Mr. Sweet. Do you know if your brother had any enemies?"

"Hundreds, I should think, but I haven't a list by me."

"I will make a list if you give me their names."

"Impossible. Their name is legion!"—he laughed rather hysterically—"and now will that do for you, Super, my wife and I would like our room to ourselves, it's a poor thing, but our own," his laugh broke out again. He was so lacking in control that Grainger felt quite uneasy about leaving him with his family, but to prolong the interview seemed likely to make him worse.

"Yes, I think that will do for the present, Mr. Sweet. I shall, of course, require you to let me know before changing your address while the investigation lasts."

"Don't worry, Super. Oddly enough I don't have the price of a ticket to South America."

Outside, in the mean, dirty street, Grainger sighed as he climbed into his car. He was tired and the family he had just seen distressed him. He reflected, as the car nosed its way back to the Yard, that both the Sweet brothers had doubtless been indignant about their own treatment as children—Pat probably used it as an excuse for his failure to engage in life—yet apparently it didn't strike him that he was meting out the same treatment, or worse, to his own two children. Dissociation is still a pretty prevalent factor in this sort of situation, he thought, although one was inclined to regard it as a pre-eminently Victorian habit; but they at least had used it to forge their own peculiarly inflexible strength. Nowadays, however, these people were all too inclined to drift in unhappy chaos on the tepid waters of the Welfare State. The problem of neurotics and psychopaths seemed, too, likely to be an increasing social problem. Protected as they must be by the laws that guard the freedom of all individuals, they were free to do harm to others which it seemed virtually impossible to prevent. Enough psychiatric treatment to enable him to change direction and harness energies to some constructive purpose might make all the difference to Patrick Sweet and his family. But people who need treatment would only very rarely volunteer for it and the state had, necessarily, no power to force them to have it; until they had incontrovertibly broken the law. Grainger sighed again, and set his mind to consider and piece together the evidence which the day's work had amassed.

The personality of the dead man was becoming increasingly obvious and postulated a wide range of suspects. None of those he had seen so far had alibis sufficient to rule them out. Some time on that Saturday morning, or possibly during the preceding night, someone had succeeded in introducing a lethal dose of barbiturate into the dead man's breakfast of coffee, sugar, cream, rolls and butter. The bitter taste of the poison suggested the sweet coffee as the obvious medium, though, owing to the activities of Mrs. Lion, this could not be proved. It was questionable whether the murderer could have relied on this removal of evidence by the charwoman, though presumably any of the Southeys, or Naomi Moore might have discovered that she meant to go down there if she had time. On the other hand the murderer would hardly have chosen that morning had he realised that Mrs. Lion would be going into Sweet's flat at a time when he might well be dying but not dead. In fact, Grainger thought, her unexpected visit may have given the murderer some very nasty moments, supposing that he got to know of it. No, it looked as though the removal of the traces of poison was purely fortuitous. The question of whether the killer had expected the bath to finish his work for him was more open; it could have been chance, or an intimate knowledge of the dead man's habits. Enough barbiturate had been found in his stomach to make it at least very probable that he would have died of this alone, supposing of course that he wasn't found in time to use a stomach pump.

Grainger was nearing the Yard now. If that safe deposit contains the sort of thing I expect, and his bank statements show a pattern that fits with it, we should be able to force this case open pretty quickly, he thought, but I'm afraid we may be held up by a multiplicity of possibles.

A constable greeted him with a message.

"There's a lady anxious to see you, sir, a Mrs. Moore. Been waiting half an hour or more."

Naomi was smartly dressed and vibrant with curiosity, and possibly Grainger suspected, also with nervousness.

"Oh, Superintendent Grainger," she said, and her light voice took him back to the interview that morning in her flat, "I'm so glad you came," she went on, "I have a theatre engagement and would have had to leave soon." Her voice was faintly reproachful, as if he should have been sitting in his room at the Yard waiting for her.

"Oh, yes, Mrs. Moore." He offered her a cigarette. "Have you thought of something else that you wanted to tell me?"

"Oh, how clever of you to guess, Superintendent! Yes, as a matter of fact I have"—she paused inhaling her cigarette almost greedily—"I wanted to tell you this morning, but—well, it's so difficult when these things involve one's friends, isn't it? I should hate to be thought disloyal or indiscreet, but I gave it a great deal of thought, indeed I've really thought of nothing else all day, and I came to the conclusion that one really isn't free to hold things back in a case of murder. I am sure you would agree with me."

"I do, indeed."

"But it is very difficult for me, and I would like you to promise me that you won't tell the people it concerns that I came to you."

"I can't give you an absolute undertaking, Mrs. Moore, but whatever you have to tell me will need to be proved and it seems likely that we should be able to do that without further reference to you."

"Thank you, Superintendent. Well, I shall have to be content with that, shan't I?" She paused again. "It's rather a long story; it all began some eight months ago when I was listening to the news on my radio and there was an SOS message. It said, 'Will Jack William Southey, last heard of twenty-five years ago in St. Ives, Cornwall, go to St. Bridgid's hospital where his wife, Margaret Anne Southey, is dangerously ill." She stopped and looked at him expectantly.

"Yes?"

"It doesn't strike you then? You see, he isn't called Jack now, but his name is William Southey, isn't it, and St. Ives is such a place for painters; I couldn't help wondering, you know. Perhaps it was just a woman's intuition. I didn't like to say anything to Mr. or Mrs. Southey, just in case there was something in my suspicion. You see, I don't myself consider bigamy a crime. So I just did nothing. But one day when Ivan and I were talking in my room, I mentioned the SOS message to him, and he was most interested and thought I was probably quite right. Naturally I told him that he mustn't think of mentioning it to anyone as it could do untold harm; as you may know, Mrs. Southey is a Catholic. And, of course, he promised most faithfully. I knew that he wouldn't think anything of bigamy either, or I wouldn't have mentioned it."

"Quite so," Grainger agreed gravely.

"Well, that's almost the end of the story, but not quite; a few months later Ivan and I were discussing another mutual friend in my room and I hesitated to hazard an opinion because I might be wrong. And then he told me I had been quite right about that SOS message. 'I just happened to be in Somerset House one day,' he said, 'and just to see if our suspicions were correct, I looked for William Southey's birth certificate and the certificates of the two marriages; and do you know, you were perfectly right;

but of course we must never think of mentioning it to them.'
And I'm sure Ivan wouldn't have meant to mention it to them,
Superintendent; he made a most particular point of it to me, he
said it might even be dangerous. But since his death I have felt
very uneasy wondering if after all perhaps he did say something.
Of course, I'm absolutely certain the Southeys would never... but
you understand my position, Superintendent?"

Grainger's manner as he answered her was so urbane that
his friends would have been warned that his mind was working
very fast.

"You did perfectly right to come and see me, Mrs. Moore. I
should like, however, to point out that the word of a dead man is
no sort of proof for these statements—I feel sure you would not
wish to be involved in a slander case." He paused. "There is also,
of course, the possibility that the possession of this information
might be dangerous to you. I say all this in order to lend weight
to my advice to you, which is to exercise an absolute discretion
on what you have told me tonight."

Naomi looked quite alarmed. "Oh yes, I will indeed,
Superintendent. I quite understand. You can rely on me not to
breathe a word to a living soul."

Grainger eyed her for a moment: "Well, thank you for coming,
Mrs. Moore. And now I expect you want to get off to your theatre
engagement."

"Oh yes, I do." She stood up. "I can't tell you what a relief it is to
get that off my chest! Now I can really give my mind to the play."

She was gone at last. Grainger pursed his lips as he made notes.
Oh dear, he said to himself, I don't know how much I'm going
to like this case. He pushed the notes away from him and leaned
back in his chair. I'm tired, he decided.

There was a token knock at the door and McGregor came bustling in very well pleased with himself.

"I have it here, sir, an' it's just what you were expecting. Dirty blackmailer the fellow was though, 'tis a rare pity he didna' come our way afore he was dead, 'twould ha' saved someone the expense o' killin' him."

"Amen to that, Mac! I'll take that lot home with me tonight."

McGregor's small blue eyes under his bushy brows regarded his superior shrewdly, "Havena' ye had enough o' today yet, sir?"

"I shall get my second wind soon," Grainger retorted. "And I want to see how that file of filth ties in with today's interviews." He began to pack his briefcase.

# NINE

S UPERINTENDENT GRAINGER, WITH HIS SCHOLAR'S STOOP, his quiet voice, the inexorably watching eyes behind his glasses, was uneasily present in many people's thoughts that night. William and Caroline, striving to pull the threads of everyday life across the chasm at their feet, found their thoughts constantly returning to that quiet man as they wondered how much he had found out about the grim tangle that had closed about them since the dead body of Ivan Sweet was lifted, dripping, from his last bath. Elaine, sitting miserably with Gideon at the theatre, found her thoughts wrenched from their preoccupation with Jonathon to the man who was hunting Sweet's murderer. Henry Meade, sitting alone with his book, for his daughter's malaise was persisting and she had gone to bed, found his thoughts wandering from the printed page back over the afternoon's interview, weighing each question and answer, probing its possible significance until, becoming impatient with the pretence of reading, he closed his book and gave his mind unreservedly to the problems that occupied it. Cecil Paignton, sitting by the dusty window of his unattractive room, an open pen in his hand, a blank page before him, thought that persecution had not stopped at Ivan's grave. The Jonas family found the wrangles of their family life made more vindictive by the anxiety that hung over them. Naomi Moore found her mind wandering from her attentive companion and the fashionable play, to Paul Grainger, trying to assess what impression she and her story had made on him. Richard Southey continually embarrassed his family, who were trying to preserve a smooth family front for the younger children's sake, by constant references to Grainger and speculation about what his next moves would be. Phoebe Sweet, trying to push her endless household chores to some sort of conclusion without waking the sleeping children, found her thoughts dwelling uneasily on the questions the alarmingly cerebral police officer had asked her husband that afternoon. Pat had blown up in one of his all too familiar tirades afterwards and flung out of the house. She had given up wondering when he would be back or where he went on these occasions. She speculated, half-unwillingly, on one of the superintendent's remarks, supposing Ivan *had* had some money to leave? Pat meanwhile was walking, lost in a familiar nightmare. The figure of Grainger was only one more phantom among those that pursued him; but he, too, made efforts to remember the sequence and details of the interview that had preceded this brainstorm. Confusion blew like a fog in and out of his mind, and only his corrosive self-hatred was clear and ever-present. Jonathon Blake, cursing his hot temper for the misery it had brought, thought also in passing of Paul Grainger, and, thinking of him, was convinced that the superintendent was not a man to fail. That Ivan Sweet's killer would be hunted down was a certainty, and, miserably, he put his mind to the fence; supposing Elaine's father... ashamed and furious with himself, he thrust the thought from him. If only she would be at the inquest tomorrow...

In his quiet, tasteful room, Paul Grainger leant back in his favourite chair and began to fill his pipe. It was late; below, the London square was already dark and the stream of cars seeking a quieter route than the big West End thoroughfares was slackening. The big trees in the square and the tall houses looking serenely down on it were claiming the night as they had been built to do when London was a city to live in, not a sprawling maze to get out of.

Peaceful, discreet, intellectual, lacking only the indefinable element of home that needs a woman's touch, Grainger's room enclosed him. Nothing remained of his brief honeymoon sixteen years ago but some photographs and jewellery in a drawer that was never opened, a pipe his wife had once given him, too burnt now for use, but still kept in the rack, a book or two they had exchanged, and one or two of the unexciting wedding presents of a war-time wedding, so long incorporated in his home that Grainger scarcely remembered now how he came by them; what had once filled his horizon with emotions of every kind had now, through long custom, lost power to affect him.

On the table beside his chair, the shaded lamp gleamed on the streaked red-brown of polished rose-wood and the decanter of wine that stood upon it shone with ruby brilliance. Paul Grainger finished filling his pipe and put the stem between his lips, gripping it with his teeth. A naturally ascetic man, he enjoyed smoking even to the minutiae that accompanied it, the smell of tobacco when he opened his pouch, and the damp feel of it between his fingers, the familiar stem between his teeth, and the acrid smoke of the match just before the first fragrant tobacco smoke. Puffing contentedly, he opened his briefcase and took out the file containing the close-hidden secrets of other people's lives that Ivan Sweet had rummaged out for his own satisfaction and profit. Almost as much for the former as the latter, Grainger thought now, as he sorted them out. Only some of this potential blackmailing material appeared to be showing a profit; perhaps the dead man had ferreted them out and secreted them away as a sort of perverted security, a source of ready money if funds were low. The detective frowned as he leafed back through the pages and the years; sniffing for skeletons in other men's cupboards had evidently been a long-established habit; there were some early entries in a younger hand whose subject matter suggested that he had been victimising his schoolfellows. During and after the last war, the records seemed to suggest that he had relied on blackmail for his livelihood. Not content with enjoying other men's wives in their absence on the battlefields that he was so careful to avoid, he had gilded his gingerbread with blackmail. These were mostly small sums, but there were enough of them to make quite a noticeable source of income. Some eighteen months after the war, however, they suddenly stopped. Grainger's practical imagination conjured up a muscular Commando husband who had perhaps frightened the verminous Sweet off this particular muck-heap. It would of course be possible to check this supposition if necessary, but he hoped it wouldn't prove to be so. To open old sores could lead to an unforeseeable chain of reactions and, as a policeman, he felt a certain responsibility that Sweet should have been at liberty to prey on these people; not that he had been in England himself at the time.

The name of an East End grocer, Isaac Goldschmidt, occurred at regular intervals from 1943 until the present day. Sweet's notes stated that this man had 'done time' when a youth and at the time he first extorted blackmail Goldschmidt had a boy reading law at Cambridge, by now doubtless a practising lawyer. His father had paid Sweet £15 a quarter for twelve years now, £720 for silence; it seemed rather unlikely that he would have taken to violence

after so long, however bitterly he felt, but he would have to be
looked into.

The luckless Cecil Paignton was represented here and had
paid a small regular sum levied on some rather pathetic letters
written to a young man. A recent and detailed account of Henry
Meade's financial status interested Grainger. There was nothing to suggest material for blackmail in this, and he suspected
that Sweet had contemplated a profitable marriage to Meade's
young daughter. There were no references, at least under their
own names, either to his brother or Naomi Moore; the Jonas's
figured, however, though singularly little detail was given, the
notes showing only the name of a school in Buckinghamshire and
the dates 1940–1944. A recent payment, in May, of £20 showed
in the profits column, and a second £20 was pencilled in against
July 30th, the date of the Southeys' party Grainger noted with
interest; he wondered if there were any particular significance
in this choice of date. Some thirty pounds in notes had been
found in the dead man's flat and he made a note to follow up the
numbers of these. He put down the papers and poured himself
a drink and, sitting back in his chair sipping it, went back in his
mind over his interview that day with the Jonas's. Hadn't the
woman remarked, when we came here eight years ago? Yes she
had; it seemed a very probable hypothesis that whatever had
happened at the Allanshurst School had precipitated the family's
move to London.

Returning to Sweet's neat and scurrilous file he sighed as he
withdrew the papers relating to the Southeys. Twenty-seven years
ago, Sweet's tiny mannered script stated, Jack William Southey,
painter, of St. Ives, Cornwall, had married Margaret Anne Howard.
Twenty-seven years ago, thought Grainger frowning, Southey's

age was difficult to assess accurately but he must surely have been a very young man, scarcely a major. Sweet had added the date of Margaret Anne Southey's death, only a few months ago, in St. Bridgid's Hospital in Cornwall. An asylum, thought the detective, why an asylum? Had she been an inmate perhaps, was that the explanation of Southey's improbable conduct? He made an entry in his own notebook and returned to Sweet's file. Six years after his first marriage, William Southey of Chelsea, London, had bigamously married Caroline Elliot. Blackmail had been levied for the past six months at the rate of £40 per month. But this was not all. For the previous month of April the profits column showed an additional payment of £50 from Caroline, and a further £50 had been pencilled in against July. Grainger's face was grim as he stared down at these facts and figures. Had Southey known Sweet was blackmailing his wife as well? It seemed to the detective improbable; his first wife after all was now dead, his motive in allowing himself to be bled by Sweet must have been rather to protect his wife and children from the knowledge of their unhappy position than to protect himself from the reach of the law. Grainger judged him to be a man not easily intimidated, had his bigamy been common knowledge in his family the detective would have expected him to tell Sweet to go ahead and do his worst rather than allow himself to be blackmailed. Not necessarily though, for had the position developed so that he was forced to retaliate by suing Sweet for extorting blackmail, he would shrink from the noisome publicity his family would have to face. There was also the very pertinent point that such publicity might wreck his career as a portrait painter. Grainger frowned as a new point occurred to him; did Southey know that his first wife was dead? Sweet would hardly have told him and he might well be in ignorance of the fact. If he imagined his first wife still to be living he would feel himself more vulnerable to blackmail even if he had taken Caroline into his confidence. It looked then as if the blackmailer, not content with drawing a safe £500 a year from the painter felt himself in so strong a position that he could bleed the woman as well. He laid down his papers and leaned his head on his hand as he tried to assess the effect of this battery of blackmail on the individual Southeys under the strong weave of family life that they presented to the world. Had the blackmailer over-reached himself at last when he attacked the woman as well? Had William and Caroline discussed the position in which they found themselves in the privacy of their studio and decided to exterminate the man who threatened their children's happiness and security? With a Catholic mother it was a virtual certainty that the children were also Catholics—to what lengths might their parents have gone to protect them from the knowledge that they were bastards? He sighed heavily, the strength of their motive either individually or combined, together with their almost unlimited opportunity was going to take a great deal of arguing away.

Methodically he repacked the papers in their file. He knocked out his pipe and began to refill it, his face battened down, his strong fingers ramming in the tobacco too tightly. Patiently he emptied it and repeated the job carefully. Breathing in the smoke, he took up his notebook again and began to make lists. They ran as follows:

| Name | Motive | Opportunity |
|------|--------|-------------|
| *William Southey*, painter. | Was being blackmailed by Sweet at rate of £500 per annum, paid monthly. Had been paying for six months at time of Sweet's death. The latter's notes state that Southey's marriage to Caroline was bigamous. Previous marriage, twenty-seven years ago to Margaret Anne Howard, died seven months before Sweet, i.e.: Nov. 1956 at St. Bridgid's hospital, Cornwall. Man of firm and decisive personality, devoted to family. | Almost unlimited, prob. aided by knowledge of dead man's habits. |
| *Caroline Elliot*, known as Mrs. Southey. Living as wife of above. Catholic. | As above. Note: children probably Catholics. | As above. |
| *Elaine Southey*, eldest daughter of above. Age 21. | Improbable, but could just conceivably have acted to protect parents and younger children. | As above. |
| *Richard Southey*, eldest son of above. Age 19. | Jealous of Sweet on account of latter's attentions to Yolande Meade. Was heard threatening to break his neck (Mrs. Jonas) on evening preceding murder. Motives as for Elaine could also conceivably apply.  *Note:* method of killing does not accord with age and temperament. | As above. |

| *Patrick Sweet*, artist, brother of dead man. | Probable heir to dead man's property. Badly in need of money. Marked bitterness and hatred towards brother. War service? History of head injury. Unbalanced personality. Unsatisfactory witness. | Was seen near Magnolia House Sat. morning (Mrs. Jonas). *Note:* check with other possible witnesses. Probable knowledge of brother's habits. |

| *Henry Meade*, retired architect. | To protect young daughter from Sweet. Disliked and distrusted dead man. Devoted widower father. Man of natural rectitude, but might go to any lengths to protect his daughter. May have suspected that Sweet meant to marry her for her expectations (quite considerable) from himself. Effective individual, quite capable of carrying out careful patient plan. | |

| *Cecil Paignton*, ? small private income. Writer. | Was being blackmailed by Sweet. Small payments over many years, but probably could ill-afford these. Sweet was in possession of unfortunate letter written to a male friend. In addition Sweet hounded him with denigratory reviews of any work he published; in these reviews he hinted at the knowledge on which he was blackmailing Paignton, who suffers noticeably from persecution mania. He is unbalanced but naturally meticulous; probably capable of the careful planning of this murder, but would his nerve hold while he carried it out? | Rather loose alibi. Needs checking. |

| *Barbara* and *Edouard Jonas*. School-teachers. | Were being blackmailed on unspecified grounds apparently connected with Allanshurst School and the years 1940–1944. *Note:* check date of removal to Magnolia Cottage. Had made first payment of blackmail monies in May of this year, £20. A further £20 had apparently been demanded for day of Southey's party (and Sweet's murder) July 30th. *Note:* check numbers on notes found in dead man's flat. Examine Jonas's financial status and of course inquire at school. If involved, probable that Mrs. Jonas would be planner, though not necessarily the executioner. | Geographically easy. Insufficient data at present. Alibis do not clear them. |
| --- | --- | --- |
| *Naomi Moore*, widow, apparently of independent means. | Apparently none, but it seems probable that she may have been involved in Sweet's affairs to some extent. She had known him a long time, and it seems possible that Sweet may have made use of her native curiosity for his own purposes. She *seems* to have liked the dead man. | Plenty in view of residence in same house and knowledge of dead man's habits. |
| *Isaac Goldschmidt*, grocer. | Had been blackmailed by Sweet at rate of £60 per year for twelve years. Had served prison sentence as a youth. Has lawyer son. Not interviewed yet. | Not known at present. |

In addition to above, various old blackmail victims showing no payments in recent years. Check these.

Paul Grainger studied these lists for some time before packing his papers away. Then he glanced at his watch and picked up the *Radio Times*. The case with all its anxieties and problems slipped gradually into the background of his mind as the inimitable, transcendental flow of a Bach Concerto slipped through his senses and wooed his mind after them. Following the theme from instrument to instrument, from variation to variation, he closed his eyes and sipped his wine and so far lost himself that he was at peace with the world for all its murderers and blackmailers.

# TEN

THE SUN SHONE THROUGH THE HIGH WINDOWS OF THE Coroner's Court and the dancing dust motes were twinkling like a diminutive galaxy of stars. Jonathon stared at them dazedly trying to digest his disappointment, the Southeys had arrived and Elaine wasn't with them. At last he forced himself to go and join them, if I can wangle an invitation, he thought...

William sat upright and very still, staring with a stern face at the great coat of arms emblazoned on the wall behind the Coroner's desk. The familiar faces he had noticed among the crowd made him feel obscurely more uncomfortable; he was very conscious of Caroline sitting beside him, and wondered how many of these people might later have to know that their marriage was—bigamy. What a revolting word it was, what the devil did it have to do with him and Caro and the children! What had all these chattering fools in their mundane respectability have to do with all they had built together? He remembered Caroline's face, her absolute trust all those years ago, before he took the plunge and married her, when she came to tell him that in six months they were to have a baby! He frowned as he lived over again the struggle of decision; yet how could any other course have been right than the one he took when he married her? Margaret lost nothing, she could no longer even recognise him...

Richard was well away on his favourite subject, history; "... of course in the Middle Ages the Crowner had a totally different function. He was appointed by the King for the direct profit of the Crown. The property of all criminals including suicides was forfeit to the Crown you see. But he had no power to arrest. Even today a man can't be arrested in a Coroner's Court even though he's been found guilty of murder. He leaves a free man and they get him on the steps outside…"

At this point rather to the relief of Richard's audience the Coroner came in through the door behind his dais, and the Coroner's officer standing by the empty jury's pews called out:

"Her Majesty's Coroner, please stand."

Richard stared with interest at the dark-suited man with the tough, intelligent, humorous face. It was not difficult to believe that he spent his life in ferreting out the truth from the mess that sudden death leaves behind it. He sat down at his desk and with a scraping of feet, the court followed suit.

"Where's the jury?" Caroline asked Richard in a whisper. "They're evidently not calling one," he replied, "means they'll probably adjourn the case until they've found out more about it."

"The case of Ivan Sweet, sir."

The Coroner nodded, sitting with pen in hand on the dais above the court. His officer led Patrick Sweet up to the witness box to the Coroner's left. Pat stumbled up the two steps into it and stood there very pale and glowering nervously.

"Take the Book," he was told. He frowned and picked a Bible off the shelf attached to the witness box.

"Say after me 'I swear by Almighty God'…"

Pat glowered and mumbled sourly, "I swear by Almighty God…"

"That the evidence I shall give…"

"That the evidence I shall give…"

"Shall be the truth, the whole truth and nothing but the truth."

"Shall be the truth, the whole truth and nothing but the truth."

The Coroner leant forward and directed a bland smile at the young man. He asked:

"You are Patrick Sweet and you reside at 156 Babbington Road, N.W.?"

"Yes, sir, so help me God." The Coroner's eyebrows rose but he made no comment.

"This is your brother Ivan Sweet who now lies dead?"

"And good riddance."

"Remarks like that are most inadvisable and you can confine yourself to answering my questions."

He paused, eyeing the witness under beetling brows.

"When did you last see your brother, Mr. Sweet?"

"I forgot to make a note of it in my diary... sir."

"Then you will kindly consult your memory, Mr. Sweet."

Patrick shrugged. "I may have seen him two or three months ago."

"Where?"

"At his flat."

"Were you paying him a friendly visit?"

"No."

"Describe your interview with him in your own words."

"I asked him for money and he refused."

"Were you in the habit of asking him for money?"

"No."

"Why did you ask him on this occasion?"

"I was even more broke than usual."

"I see. What manner of man was your brother?"

"I cannot answer that question in language you would pass... sir."

"What was his occupation?"

"Search me."

"Answer my question, Mr. Sweet."

"Very well. Living off other people, probably women. Writing, acting, on and off the stage, what he called painting."

The Coroner stopped writing to direct a hard stare at the witness, then he asked:

"Did your brother enjoy good health?"

"I imagine so."

"Was he in the habit of taking drugs?"

"I never heard him mention it."

"Was he a man likely to take his own life?"

"Good God, no!"

"Was he under medical treatment?"

"I have no idea."

"Was he a man to make enemies?"

"And how! Yes, he most certainly was."

"On the night of July 30th you were attending a party at the house where your brother was living. I understand you went down to fetch him. Will you describe to the court what happened?"

The question appeared to discomfort Patrick. However, he told his tale with reasonable clarity and was stood down.

William Southey got up as the Coroner's officer came towards him and walked to the witness box. He stood there, tall and austere, waiting to be questioned. He was sworn in.

"I understand you were holding a party at your residence on the night of Saturday, July 30th?"

"Yes, sir."

"You asked Mr. Patrick Sweet to fetch his brother who had accepted an invitation to attend but had not arrived?"

"That is so."

"Will you describe to the court in your own words what happened when you yourself went down to investigate after Mr. Patrick Sweet returned?"

"Yes, sir. Mr. Jonathon Blake offered to accompany me as we anticipated mending a fuse and possibly a washer and I wanted someone to hold a torch for me. We went straight down, the fuse boxes are in the basement. There was water as Sweet had said, on the floor of the passage leading to the bathroom. By the light of the torch we could see that it was coming from under the bathroom door. There is a step there over which it was flowing which accounted for the dripping sound. I called Mr. Ivan Sweet's name, but there was no reply and I tried the door. It was locked and I decided that we had better investigate this before attending to the fuse. It seemed to me possible that Sweet might have had a seizure in his bath. The door was very stout and we had to fetch an axe before we were able to break it in. I shone the torch inside. The floor was under water and one of the taps was running. It was the hot tap. I shone the torch into the bath and saw Mr. Ivan Sweet in it. He was under water. No bubbles were rising. Mr. Blake and I hauled him out at once and laid him on the floor where we took turns in giving him artificial respiration. We persisted for some time but there was no sign of life. Perhaps it is relevant that Mr. Blake is a medical student. I asked him to continue with the artificial respiration and propped up the torch to give some light. I then ran upstairs to the telephone in the hall to call a doctor. Our own doctor was away on holiday or he would have been at the party. I rang his locum but he was out on a case. I put down the receiver and considered my course of action. Although Mr. Sweet appeared to be dead I decided that time might still be vital, so I wasted no time trying to find another doctor but dialled 999 and asked for the police. I explained the situation and they promised to be round in a few minutes with a doctor. I returned to Mr. Blake and took over from him. There was still no sign of life. The police were as good as their word and soon as they arrived I handed Mr. Sweet over to their police surgeon and got permission for Mr. Blake and myself to mend the fuse. When this was done we returned to the bathroom. The doctor confirmed that Mr. Sweet was dead and Mr. Blake and I made a statement to the police. I then asked if I could go and inform my guests of what had happened. Permission for this was given and I was asked to keep them in the house until the police had questioned them."

"Thank you, Mr. Southey. That was admirably clear. Mr. Ivan Sweet was your tenant?"

"Yes, sir."

"How long had he been so?"

"For nine months."

"Was he a satisfactory tenant?"

"Perfectly."

"What manner of man was he, Mr. Southey?"

For the first time the painter hesitated, but only for a second.

"He was not a friend, sir, merely a tenant."

"Quite so, but you must have formed some impression of him."

"I was not particularly drawn to him, but he was, as I have said, a perfectly satisfactory tenant."

"Did you ever hear him complain of his health?"

"No."

"Have you any idea whether he was in the habit of taking sleeping pills?"

"I'm afraid I have no idea, sir."

"He was not as far as you know under doctor's orders?"

"Not as far as I know."

"Although he was not a friend, he received an invitation to your party?"

"It was a very large party, in honour of my daughter's twenty-first birthday. My wife felt it would be discourteous not to invite him as he lived in the house and we had a few mutual friends among the guests."

"I see. Thank you, Mr. Southey. That's all I need ask you. Next witness, please."

Jonathon replaced William in the witness box and the Coroner took him over his story which tallied with that told by the painter. He elicited the fact that the dead man had been unknown to the young medical student.

The police surgeon was then called.

"You examined Mr. Ivan Sweet at Magnolia House, South Hill, on Saturday night, July 30th?"

"I did, sir."

"What were your findings?"

"I examined the body and found the man to be dead. There were no external signs of violence. The face was cyanosed and there was froth in his mouth, but from an external examination it was not possible to assign a cause of death. Rigor had not yet set in."

"Were you able to make an estimate of how long he had been dead?"

"I should say between seven and twelve hours, sir. It is difficult to be more definite as the warmth of the bath may have delayed the onset of rigor. It was still lukewarm when I arrived, I understand the hot tap had been running when the man was found."

"Thank you, Doctor. I'll take Dr. James now."

The pathologist rose and installed his burly form in the witness box. He was sworn in.

"You made an examination for me in this case, what were your findings?"

"The body was that of a well-nourished young man and there were no external signs of violence. The air passages were filled with frothy fluid and the lungs were filled with fluid and very congested. To a lesser extent all organs were congested and there were many small haemorrhages due to anoxia. Clearly the immediate cause of death was asphyxia due to drowning. There were no signs of natural disease."

"I understand that certain organs and other specimens were removed for analysis?"

"Yes, sir."

"Thank you, Dr. James, that's all I need ask you. Call the analyst, please."

"You received Mr. Sweet's stomach and other organs for analysis?" the Coroner asked the tall thin man in the witness box.

"Yes, sir, they were delivered to me yesterday in sealed and labelled containers."

"Is your analysis now complete?"

"Yes, sir."

"What was found?"

"Considerable quantities of sodium amytal were recovered from the stomach and to a lesser extent from the upper small intestine. There were also traces in the liver and brain."

"Did these quantities amount to a poisonous dose?"

"Many times the safe dose were recovered, sir."

"Thank you, Doctor, then I need not detain you. I will take the evidence of Mr. Grainger."

Paul Grainger took the stand and was sworn in.

"What have your investigations into this case shown so far?"

"On the night of Saturday, July 30th, I went to Magnolia House as the result of a telephone call from the owner, Mr. William Southey. I arrived with my sergeant at 10.40 p.m. The police surgeon had arrived immediately before us and had already ascertained that Mr. Ivan Sweet was dead. I examined the room and the bath in which Mr. Sweet had been discovered and noted that the bath overflow pipe was partially blocked by a large soft sponge which had got sucked into the hole. The appearances suggested that this was accidental. This was the reason for the flooding which the bath had caused. The tap which Mr. Southey and Mr. Blake told me had been running when they found the body had been turned off. I found no evidence pointing to suicide. I took statements from Mr. Southey and Mr. Blake and from Mr. Patrick Sweet, the dead man's brother. I telephoned for assistance from the Special Departments to take photographs and test for finger-prints. When this was completed, the body was dispatched to the mortuary and the dead man's flat sealed after a preliminary search. My sergeant meanwhile had taken down the names and addresses of all those present in the house that night. Investigations are still continuing."

"As far as you are concerned, then, the story is not yet clear how Mr. Sweet came to take a fatal dose of sodium amytal?"

"No, sir, it is not yet clear."

"Well, in that case, I shall adjourn this inquest pending further evidence. Would two weeks from this date be suitable?"

"Yes, sir."

"That will be Tuesday, August 17th. Next case, please."

# ELEVEN

GRAINGER PARKED HIS CAR AND WALKED IN THROUGH THE double doors of the bank. He leant over the counter and in the traditional whisper reserved for banks and churches, informed the cashier that he had an appointment with the manager. He was ushered into the dark well-polished waiting-room for a few minutes before he gained the inner sanctum where an even-featured man with neatly brushed iron-grey hair rose from a large desk to greet him with professional urbanity. The manager was suave and well-groomed, and probably, thought Grainger, adept in reticence.

"Good afternoon, Superintendent. Do sit down. What is it that I can do for you?"

"You could help me very much if you will, sir. As you may know one of your customers has recently met his death in very suspicious circumstances. A Mr. Ivan Sweet."

A wooden look descended over the manager's face though his pleasant smile remained as though painted there.

"Mr. Ivan Sweet. Hmm, yes." He rang a bell and a bank clerk appeared. "Will you fetch me the file for Mr. Ivan Sweet please, Barnes?"

"Yes, sir." The young man laid it before him a moment later.

"Thank you, Barnes." He nodded a dismissal, and opened the file. His eye ran quickly over the columns but his face gave no indication of what they conveyed to him.

"And what particularly did you want to know, Superintendent?" he asked. His tone suggested that Grainger showed a regrettable tendency to vulgar curiosity.

"Mr. Sweet's financial affairs are very far from clear, sir. He does not appear to have held regular paid employment at any time although he was accustomed to live in some degree of comfort. It occurs to me that he may have enjoyed a private income and it would greatly assist my inquiries to know this. The question of his heir is also relevant of course. We understand he left no will so any property he may have possessed presumably now belongs to his next of kin."

"I see. Yes. Well, in the circumstances I think I am at liberty to tell you that Mr. Sweet did hold various shares and properties that afforded him a private income."

"A substantial income?"

The manager pursed his lips, "That, of course, is a matter of interpretation, but it was certainly quite sufficient for a young man with no family ties."

"You would say then that he had no cause for financial worries?"

"Well, we find, Superintendent, that some of our substantial clients are more disposed to worry about their finances than those who have perhaps more reason to do so. However, I do not myself see that Mr. Sweet had any particular reason to be anxious."

"Was he an old-established client—had his family banked with you before him?"

"No. No, as a matter of fact he wasn't. He opened his account with us, let me see"—he consulted the file—"oh, yes, here we are, in 1947."

Grainger noted the date. "And can you give me some guide as to the amount of his annual income, in round figures you know?"

"Well, Superintendent," the manager demurred, "we do regard the giving of that sort of information as a breach of our customer's confidence, you know."

"I am of course aware of that, sir, and if necessary I could doubtless obtain sufficient information from the tax inspector who handled his affairs, but it would be a great convenience if you could see your way to helping me; particularly it would save time, and time, as you will understand, is of very great moment to us in these first days of an investigation while the tracks are still fresh which may lead us to the killer." His eyes behind the horn-rimmed glasses met the other man's as he added, "Perhaps you will feel more free to assist me if I take you into my confidence and inform you that Mr. Sweet kept a record of profits obtained by blackmail. The information which he used to extort this money is also in our hands."

The manager's face underwent a radical change; Grainger was no longer the rather impertinent questioner it was his duty to resist. Two pillars of society were now united against the blackmailer.

"Ah. Thank you, Superintendent; that of course puts a totally different complexion on the matter." He became confidential, "I'm sure you understand, Superintendent Grainger, that our position forces us to reticence about our client's affairs, but in a case like this of course… Now let me see what might be of assistance to you." He picked up the file and opened it out on his desk.

"First the figure you wished to know; these things fluctuate somewhat naturally—as we all know—although these are excellent securities, in fact…" He looked up at the detective with a smile, "I take it that opinions are also useful to you?"

Grainger smiled back, "Oh, very useful indeed, sir."

"Well, we have some experience in these matters, of course, and it did strike me as rather improbable that Mr. Sweet would have been likely to select this type of security himself... I would have expected something rather more—speculative. I also received the impression, for what it's worth, that when Mr. Sweet first opened his account with us, he was possibly not accustomed to a regular income. In fact a recent inheritance suggested itself to me. But I must emphasise, of course, that this is the merest supposition."

"I quite understand. I am most grateful for any such impressions. If I may say so, a man of your experience would obviously be in a position to form some very shrewd judgments of your clients from a financial standpoint, and of course the financial angle is one which can hardly be over-emphasised in my work." He smiled. "Money may not be the root of all evil, but it is certainly at the bottom of a great deal of crime."

The bank manager nodded in wholehearted agreement. "I could hardly agree with you more. Yes, indeed." He looked across at Grainger with approval: "Banking, you know, is very far from being devoid of human interest; people who regard it as a great deal of dull casting of figures have no idea of the tales these figures can tell. I doubt if any diary is as detailed and complete a record of the ups and downs of everyday life as an account book. But I digress. Mr. Sweet has for the past nine years enjoyed an income, subject to tax of course, of some nine hundred pounds a year. Though this is not by some standards large, you will appreciate that it represents a very comfortable sum invested to bring this return in these days. I must confess that it somewhat surprised me that Mr. Sweet made no attempt at any time to realise his capital. Young people are so often tempted to do this, but I think perhaps he possessed a streak of caution which prompted him to leave his nest-egg as it was. A very prudent decision." He turned over the pages of the file.

"He made various payments at irregular intervals but these do not suggest blackmail to me, rather I should say casual employment, possibly of a literary nature."

Grainger smiled, "You are quite right. The blackmail payments were made in cash of course and were doubtless a great convenience to him as they would not have to be declared. May I ask whether he drew cheques such as self cheques and others to meet recurrent expenses such as rent, etc., in a regular pattern?"

"No. No, I was going to mention that. The pattern of withdrawals of this kind is usually very clear of course, but not in this case. In fact these figures show that Mr. Sweet must have had an additional source of income which did not pass through his account with us. It is of course possible that he had a second account at another bank."

"No. We have already looked into that, but this was his only account. May I ask whether Sweet lodged any private papers with you?"

"No, we held nothing of that sort for him at all. You mentioned I think that no will has been found?"

"No. It seems likely that he didn't make one."

"Frankly, it would not surprise me. May I inquire whether any relatives have been traced?"

"Oh yes, there is a brother."

"Oh, is there? A brother, well, hmm." The bank manager permitted his interest to show, but it was Grainger's turn not to be drawn. He smiled the pleasant smile with which he was wont to take the sting out of a necessary withdrawal or an obnoxious question, and said:

"Well, sir, I am most grateful to you. As you yourself remarked, figures correctly interpreted can tell us so much and both your factual information and your impressions have been most valuable in filling in some of the details of my case. As you will readily understand, we need to build up a very complete picture of a man who dies in such circumstances as Mr. Sweet."

"There must be considerable interest to be found in the task. Would it be impermissibly curious to ask the manner of his death?"

"No, indeed. It will be in the evening papers, the inquest was held this morning. Sweet had taken a fatal dose of sodium amytal and was found dead in his bath."

"Hmm. Well I shall follow your case with great interest."

Grainger walked thoughtfully to the square where his car was parked, unlocked it and sat down to make notes of the interview. This done he lit his pipe and glanced at his watch. It was ten to three and very hot, the plane trees in the square were limp and dusty and most people were moving in the somnambulistic way that heat engenders; his eyes idly followed two shapely girls, bouncing along on newly acquired high heels and chattering with light-hearted vivacity in sharp contrast to the older people about them, giving these by comparison a worn, used look. The heat which reveals all women in the few garments which then adorn their various shapes, displayed these two young things resplend-ent as summer flowers, and for a moment he remembered, not his wife whom he had known only in a war-time winter, but his mother, in the fly-away clothes that had made her look so young and pretty. For the first time he felt an impulse of tolerance for her flighty habits that had endowed him with an innate distrust of pretty women. His wife had died before she had a chance to disabuse him of this, and into his grief had come a sense of fate, as though he had not been intended to marry and fate had punished him for flying in its face.

The two girls, their gay frocks blowing in a flicker of summer breeze against their ripe young bodies, holding their light-hearted hats with still childish fingers dressed up in lace, disappeared through the wide doors of a big store. Feeling unaccountably younger, Paul Grainger put his car into gear and turned its nose for the East End.

He drove through London's alternating vistas of squalor and occasional grace or grandeur until the streets grew unrelievedly dirtier and meaner, while the trees and green spaces became fewer and fewer. Ragged urchins played in the streets for lack of grass to play on; small sisters snatched smaller brothers out of the path of lorries and cars and all stared sullenly at the gleaming cellulose bowling down their playgrounds. A few of the bolder threw stones. Teddy-boys dressed with the gross and pathetic artistry of their kind, stood about on the pavements and watched him go past with deadpan faces under the conventional long haircut. Many of the adolescent girls were attractive and looked happier—and busier. Among them the early-ripe Jewish women with their bold features and blue-black hair, often tied up in the provocative horsetail, and the smart-as-paint clothes that displayed their female bodies stood out in pungent feminine appeal. There was an exciting exoticism about them, an eastern voluptuousness foreign to our northern streets, an animal consciousness of body that drew even the most unwilling eye. Their vitality was superb, less so their voices. Grainger drove on in a curiously detached mood through which visual impressions seemed to break with unaccustomed vividness; a jet plane screamed across the sky above the mean house-tops, drowning the lesser clamour of the street. He saw the upturned faces of the children and images chased through his mind to pile into the mushroom-shaped cloud whose shadow now hangs above all human lives, the final argument posed to quarrelsome mankind, a spectre as real and immediate to the sleek politician, the materialistic bureaucrat, the ancient pomp of privilege, as to Tommy Atkins in his little brick house and his wife holding the baby closer as the screaming plane tears by. His mind swung at a tangent into the invigorating vistas of space; if *homo sapiens* learnt co-operation enough to survive, what new worlds might not lie open to his ingenious mind! If the will to live proved strong enough, where might he not go, this amazing, courageous, defenceless little biped!

Sucking absently at his empty pipe, he drove more slowly now, looking for the thoroughfare where he expected to find Isaac Goldschmidt, grocer. He found the street and reversed to turn down it. His eye ran along the shop-fronts—ah, here it was, a small independent grocer, seemingly quite flourishing. He drove beyond it, parked the car and walked back. The shop was full of people and heavily accented conversation; he felt rather uncomfortably conspicuous as he walked in and numerous pairs of dark eyes swivelled at him, ran a dispassionate glance over him from head to feet and returned without interruption to their conversation. The grocer, an elderly Jew of sparrow-like build and his solidly voluminous wife were busily and efficiently serving their customers to the accompaniment of innumerable details of family life.

Anxious to get the old man alone without revealing the damaging words 'police investigation', Grainger waited until

Goldschmidt left the counter and then accosted him quietly as he
made for his store-room. The old Jew gave him a sharp glance but
showed him without demur into a small parlour behind the shop.

Grainger stood in the little room looking round him. It was
plastered with photographs of Goldschmidt's son; at Cambridge
in his commoner's gown, and again in his B.A. gown. He next
appeared in a group photograph on Law Finals Day. The pictorial
record continued with a large shiny print of a very well-turned-
out bridal pair and several unframed flash photographs of what
seemed to have been a gay and crowded wedding breakfast. A
studio portrait of three small Goldschmidt grandsons brought it
up to date. Paul Grainger sighed as he looked round the unpreten-
tious little parlour which looked as if it hadn't changed for thirty
years, and his mind travelled to William Southey with his large
family and his fine pictures; to the elderly, reserved Henry Meade
and his pretty daughter; to the plump little Cecil Paignton living
quietly in his private hell; to Patrick Sweet's young wife and her
two tiny children; to worried wives paying a blackmailer out of
a soldier's pay and he wished it was Ivan Sweet and not his killer
that he had been set to hunt down.

Isaac Goldschmidt returned; he took off his white apron and
folded it over a chair. His dark eyes looked out of a stern face at
Grainger.

"Who are you?" he asked.

The superintendent handed the old man his card. The Jew
read it with an unmoved face.

"What did you want to know?"

"Mr. Ivan Sweet had been blackmailing you for a good many
years?"

"Did he tell you that?"

"I have seen records of the sums you paid him and I know the grounds on which he demanded these."

"If you know that, you know also that you have nothing against me," riposted the Jew immediately. "I served my full sentence, with remissions for good behaviour"—the sibilant words were thick on his tongue—"forty years ago. I would never have paid money to this vampire"—he spat the word—"but that I did not wish my son to know." His eyes wandered to the photographs on the wall.

"Perhaps you would like to know that I share your opinion of Mr. Sweet and as you say that sentence is a closed chapter and very old history. It is not with that that I am concerned."

"Then why did you wish to see me, Superintendent?"

"I wish to know when you last saw Mr. Sweet."

The old man allowed his venom to show on his face.

"My relations with this Mr. Sweet were not of a social character, Superintendent. I would never have been in his hands at all if I had not been foolish enough to allow him credit at my shop during the war when he was down and out. How he discovered this old trouble of mine I do not know, but he used his knowledge first to escape from paying me the monies that he owed me and later to extort money from me. I sent this to an accommodation address at regular intervals and told him to keep out of my way if he wished me to continue it. I have not seen him for"—he shrugged—"perhaps ten years."

"You are not aware then that Mr. Sweet is dead?"

"Dead?" The old man's face became suddenly inscrutable. "No," he said slowly, "I did not know that he was dead. I will not pretend that it is not good news. This explains your visit."

He looked up at the police officer and said with emphasis, "If you imagine that I would risk my neck to kill that man after paying him money all these years, you are unrealistic. Certainly he is better dead, but I am not your man, Superintendent."

"I am glad to hear you say so, Mr. Goldschmidt, but you will understand that I shall require an account of your movements on the day he died."

"But I do not know on which day he died."

"Quite so. It was last Saturday, July 30th."

"Last Saturday… My shop was closed; as you must be aware, I am a Jew. I spent the morning in here, Superintendent, with my books. In the afternoon I took my wife to Hyde Park; we sat in the sun and listened to the band playing. We had a late tea at the Corner House and returned home afterwards. I played a little on my piano"—he nodded at an ancient but well-cared-for instrument against the wall—"and we retired to bed."

"Was your wife in the house with you during the morning?"

"No. She paid a visit to a friend whose boy is sick."

"So there is no one to corroborate your statement that you spent the morning in this room?"

"No. There is no one. My wife left soon after breakfast and returned at lunch-time." His dark eyes met the detective's with sober melancholy.

"Thank you, Mr. Goldschmidt, that is all I want to know, except the accommodation address to which you sent the money."

"I can tell you that from memory if you like to write it down." Grainger noted the address and took his leave, retiring as inconspicuously as possible through the crowded shop.

# TWELVE

How does one get on with anything, Caroline thought helplessly, when the future seems to hang on a thread above an abyss? She wondered where William had gone and what he was doing. If he means to paint he'll be changing into his working clothes. Standing there, in the empty hall, imagining him upstairs in the studio, alone, it came to her what she must do. She went into the kitchen and prepared a coffee-tray.

William was in the studio, but he was not painting. He sat at his desk with his head in his hands and she felt the cold weight of fear within her increase and somewhere deep down inside her she began to shiver uncontrollably.

William raised his head and looked at her out of hollow eyes; he made an attempt to smile and said:

"I must get started, mustn't I?"

"Have a cup of coffee first." Caroline strove to make her voice sound natural against the weights that hung on her vocal cords.

She watched him while he took his pipe out of his pocket and began to fill it. His eyes were on his hands. There was a silence. Caroline gulped down the black bitter coffee with what seemed to her a reverberating noise, her heart pounding in her chest so that she was quite surprised it didn't shake her in her chair. It seemed impossible to draw enough breath into her lungs. She tightened her jaw so that the shivering wouldn't show on her face.

"Will?" she got out suddenly, and was appalled that she had actually spoken. But there was no going back now. William had raised his head and was looking at her expectantly. She forced her voice past the obstruction in her throat and it sounded in her ears like the voice of a stranger.

"Will, I think it's time I told you that I know about Margaret."

He stared at her from what seemed an enormous distance, his face so stripped of flesh that she seemed to see the skull beneath it, his eyes sunk in the bony hollows looking out at her as from a vortex of despair.

"You know?" His strangled voice could hardly leave his throat.

He buried his face in his hands again, rubbing his brows to and fro on the palms of his hands.

"I wanted you never to know," he said in a muffled voice. Caroline got up and stood behind him, raising his head with her hands so that it leaned against her breast.

"Poor Will," she said almost absently, "poor Will."

Despite the storm it must provoke there had been peace in breaking that silence at last. Whatever was to follow now would surely give the quietus to the haggard preoccupation with conjecture that made all peace impossible.

She ran a tentative hand through his hair, seeing him double, her dear, trustworthy Will—a stranger who was another woman's husband.

"I don't know what made you do it, but—it must have cost you a lot to carry it alone all these years."

"Oh, God!" he said. He reached up a hand for her. "Come and sit down, my darling, and let's talk now that we blessedly can. Not that talking can undo what's done…"

"It's a relief, anyway."

"A relief! I can't tell you what a relief it is. I've been round and round and over and over it, again and again, and there was never any answer, any way out that would put it right for you and the children." He looked at her almost shyly and said, "I knew I ought to wish undone—that night that committed us. But I couldn't, Caro, I couldn't! Whatever man or priest may say, it was inevitable and right. Right as few things ever are in this sorry life. But that's all very well for me. I'm not a Catholic and though I was break-ing the law of the land I wasn't breaking any laws of my own... Margaret was beyond any help that I or anyone else could give her... When I went to visit her in the asylum—"

Caroline gave a gasp.

"In the asylum?" she echoed.

"Yes, but of course, you don't know... oh, love, perhaps you might think it offers some little extenuation for what I've done. Margaret was mad. At the time you and I met she had been in an asylum, certified, for five years. She was completely, hopelessly insane. I used to go and visit her in those terrible years before I met you and she didn't even know me. You can't imagine what it was like, what she had become, she was scarcely human... It began when we had been married only a few weeks... we were both very young, just over twenty... First it was only nightmare patches, and then for a few days or a few weeks she'd be herself again, and I, poor ignorant fool that I was, imagined that I could cure her, hold her to the sanity we both longed for. But always the nightmare returned and I never knew what to guard against next; she used to set fire to our studio, scatter filth on our bed and behave, oh, with the most fantastic obscenity. And then suddenly it would all be over and we would try to pick up the threads of ordinary life again. We were always desperately poor, because the first thing she did every time was to destroy my pictures, and, of course, whenever I got a commission I didn't know when to arrange sittings because it was so often impossible. But she was so piteous in between that I couldn't give up trying to help her. During one of these times she told me what I hadn't known before, that her mother was in Broadmoor for murdering her father... I didn't think I was a coward, but fear lived with me night and day after that and I could find no way of shaking it off... And so it went on until one hot summer night, there was a full moon I remember... she was always worse when the moon was full... she'd been raging and shrieking obscenities and hurling herself about all day, she'd ripped every canvas she could lay hands on and set fire to the bed; I was at my wits' end; a dozen times an hour I nearly went out and phoned for help, but somehow I managed to resist the temptation, and then in the small hours she suddenly collapsed and slept. I sat down and looked at her, her mouth was open and she was snoring loudly, a ghastly shrilling sound. Even that sounded mad to me by then. I looked round the shambles of our studio and told myself that I must begin clearing up, but I sat on and in the end I must have fallen asleep. When I woke her face was pressed into mine and her fingers were at my throat... she always used to say that's how she'd do it and I expect she would have managed, she was a little thing but her strength at such times was unbelievable. Fortunately she shrieked and gibbered all the while and a nice old chap who used to paint boats came up from his studio downstairs, fearing another fire, and he heard her gibbering about throttling the breath out of my foul body... He very bravely came in and managed to pull her off. She tore his face and throat and ripped his trousers but he hung on until I'd recovered enough to help him... We had to tie her up, poor soul, while he fetched the police and she was certified by two doctors and taken off to the asylum… I often went to see her there, but she deteriorated with the most ghastly rapidity…"

"Oh, my poor darling, and I never knew! My poor, poor Will!"

He took her hands and laid them on his face. After a while he went on,

"I left Cornwall in the end and came up to London and set myself paint and paint and forget about it all. I was still very young. And then five years later I met you, my darling, that day at the Academy, remember?"

"I remember. I thought I'd never seen anything so lovely as your painting hanging there…"

"And I thought I'd never seen anything so lovely as you, look-ing up at it."

"And we talked and talked… and had lunch together there… oh, I remember!"

"And I told myself there was no harm in enjoying each other's company, because I would be able to see that it never went any further than that… But soon I was living for the times when I saw you, and I knew that, though we never mentioned it, you felt as I did. And I knew that I would have to tell you about Margaret and that then I would never see you again… I thought, at least I'll have a portrait of you and I began to paint you…" His eyes went up to the portrait on the wall of the young Caroline. "How I longed all day for those sittings, just the two of us in my studio and the world outside going its way while we talked about every-thing under the sun and I painted as I had never painted before, and we drank coffee and red wine out of Italian bottles and ate French bread and Gruyère cheese and black figs and peaches… I used to hunt the stalls for the things that would please you for our midnight suppers!… and then one night the portrait was finished, and I kissed you, love, and our bodies spoke and wouldn't be gainsaid…" He stopped speaking and Caroline broke in at once:

"Darling, that was no more your fault than mine… and however wrong it was, I never want to forget that night."

"Caro, you can say that now?"

Caroline shook her head, "I shouldn't, I know, but it's the truth. Go on with what you were telling me, Will."

He frowned.

"After that I knew I had to tell you. Every day I swore I would do it before nightfall, and every day I still hadn't spoken… And then one evening you came and told me that we were going to have a baby. And I took the law into my own hands and did what I had been longing to do, made you my wife." He took her hands and held them tightly between his own.

"And that was twenty years ago. They've been such good years, Caro… and now, because I couldn't bring myself to give you up, I've brought you to this… married to a bigamist and all our children, bastards in the eyes of the law."

"They must never know," said Caroline. She walked away from him, over to the window.

"When all this is over"—she looked at him with agonised anxiety—"it will all be over for us, won't it, Will, this beastly business of Ivan Sweet's death I mean?"

His nod brought her less comfort than she had hoped for. She wrenched her mind from the brink of this quagmire and went on: "You—you've no idea what's become of her?" William shook his head. "No, Caro, I haven't. I'm afraid after I—married you, I tried to pretend she had never existed." He shivered and his face was haunted as he said:

"I dread to think what she must be like by now." They were both silent, their thoughts engulfed by the monstrosity of madness.

Caroline said suddenly, "Ivan Sweet was involved in all this, wasn't he, Will?"

She couldn't hide those uncontrollable shivers now.

"How did you know?" His voice had no tone. Caroline found herself staring at him; she dropped her eyes. "He started dropping hints. I laughed at him—I thought it was just—his nasty mind. But he went on... Then one day Naomi made an odd remark. I told myself it was just coincidence... but I began to wonder. Then one day Sweet asked me to lend him twenty pounds. I told him it was out of the question and then he became very unpleasant. He remarked that he was doing a great deal for me and it was time I saw my way to doing something for him. He had always, he said, thought me such a devoted mother, I would be lending it for the children's sake. I was angry then and asked what my children could possibly have to do with it, and he gave a nasty laugh and said they had everything to do with it and he was sure I could spare him twenty pounds if I thought enough about it. He asked me if I had ever been down to Somerset House. I said no, I'd never had any reason to go. He said no? Well he'd recommend a visit. I would certainly find it interesting."

"And you went?"

"I had to, Will."

"Yes. Of course."

"You remember that day I had a migraine and went to bed?"

"You've known ever since then?"

"Yes." Their eyes met despairingly. "The next day he asked me to lend him fifty pounds. I took it out of my savings book."

William buried his head in his hands. "You, too. Oh God, it's worse than I thought. Caro, for God's sake don't let the police know this. It's bad enough as it is."

Out in the garden the baby began to cry. Caroline looked at her watch, "I must get lunch," she said; her lips were white and she was still shivering.

"How are we going to face the others when they come in tonight?" she asked. She got up unsteadily. "I can't believe this is happening to us. I keep thinking I'll wake up soon and know at last that it's a ghastly dream"—her voice broke.

"Whatever happens, it can't go on like this," said Will heavily; "one way or another it has to end sometime."

There was a knock at the door and Mrs. Lion came in, the baby in her arms. "It's raining, drat it," she said, "so I brought 'im in. I thought as maybe you was busy and 'adn't noticed."

"Oh, thank you, Mrs. Lion." Caroline took the baby from her. "No, you're quite right, I hadn't noticed."

# THIRTEEN

B Y THE TIME DAWN BROKE GRAINGER AND MCGREGOR HAD
already reached Stonehenge.

"Let's pull in for a few moments and drink some of that tea,"
said Grainger, yawning and trying to stretch his legs in the con-
fined space of the car.

"Aye, I could do wi' a cup o' tea," McGregor yawned in his turn.

"Yonder's the dawn breakin'," he remarked, looking out of
the window; he wound it down and breathed in the fresh sweet
air. "It's guid!"

Grainger smiled at the big Scotsman's pleasure.

"Whenever I find myself up at this time I wonder why I don't
do it every day," he remarked, "there's nothing quite like it."

McGregor was pouring tea into two big beakers, "Aye," he
agreed, "'tis the flesh that's weak."

Both men sipped their tea with enjoyment.

"Yon's a mighty queer affair. Kind of a church for the stone-age
fellows, wasna' that it?"

"Yes, they came here to worship. From a great distance many
of them." Grainger stared across at the circle of stones through his
glasses, his sandy lashes protecting his eyes against the rising sun.

"Those stones must have seen some blood in their time, Mac."

"Human sacrifice?"

"Mmm. Odd to imagine the scene as it must have been then,
isn't it? Not that one can, of course, it's too long ago…" He stared

at the monster stones silhouetted against the fast lightening sky; the short turf that flowed to their grey feet grew greener moment by moment and the rising sun blazed in every dew-drop—a green and sparkling carpet in this ancient temple, but the grey monoliths squatted, hunched and inscrutable on the plain, rags of mist clinging to their shoulders as one more dawn broke over them. It must take a century to mark those granite faces, Grainger thought.

"Some of those stones are supposed to have been brought by sea from Milford in Wales," he told the sergeant. "Incredible, isn't it?"

"It is that! I'd rather crack this case than man-handle those stones."

Grainger sighed, "Yes, this case. That a gentle hint about this wandering in a distant stone age, Mac?" He settled back in his seat as the other man put the car into gear. "I wonder what the asylum will have to tell us about this poor woman, Margaret Southey?" he continued after a moment. "If she was an inmate it might help to explain Southey's behaviour. He's not my idea of a bigamist. If that was the reason it would be easier to understand. In fact it would be rather ironic, for thanks to A. P. Herbert, he could have got a divorce if it had happened later."

"Aye, it'd be bad luck if that was the way of it. But things being as they are, he had a mighty strong motive for shutting Sweet's mouth."

Grainger nodded, "Yes, Mac, that's only too true. But he's not alone in the field. It would have suited a whole lot of people to shut Sweet's mouth. And the whole Southey household's opportunity was almost too ample."

"Hrrmph. It's a considerable pity we canna' trace a recent purchase of sodium amytal back to any of 'em. Someone must have amassed a store of it."

"Yes, unfortunately that's only too easy nowadays, so many people have sleeping tablets prescribed at some time or another. I wish we could make more progress on how it was introduced into his food and drink. The coffee seems the obvious medium, but how was it done? It would be no good mixing it with the dry coffee or sugar, which could have been done any time of course, but there wouldn't have been a sufficient concentration to kill him. No. Either someone went down there that morning and actually added it to his cup, or it was somehow added to the cream. But if the latter, they'd have to be sure he'd finish it, or it wouldn't have done the trick."

"A carton of cream to a pint o' coffee! But I wouldna' be surprised if he was an extravagant sort o' chap. I meant to ask ye, what did his bank manager have to say?"

"Very much what we predicated. He had a private income of nine hundred pounds a year or thereabouts. It takes a tidy sum to show that sort of return these days."

The Scotsman was duly impressed. "Wonder how much that brother of his knew about that? Make a deal o' difference to his set-up, that would."

"It would indeed. Though Ivan may well have kept it a pretty closely guarded secret from a borrowing brother. But we shall have to see if we can't shake him on that categorical ignorance of his. I'm interested in where that money came from; his bank manager couldn't tell me. I'm going to put you on to that, Mac, when we get back to town. We may have to go the long way round, but we'll play a hunch first. I think Somerset House might help us again; I want you to look into the will of a certain Mildred Price. I've a feeling she may give us our answer. If so we might have new applicants for our lists."

"I could do without any additions to our list of suspects," McGregor remarked. "As it is we've the whole Southey family, that balmy wee writer, the dead man's brother, Mr. Meade and those folks in the cottage next door all on the spot that morning. Oh, yes, I had something for you about the Jonas's; their financial state isna' too happy. I wouldna' say they could afford to pay hush money; that pretty boy Edouard speculates on the Stock Exchange."

"Is that so? Hmm, that's good work. I wish I knew what it was Sweet was holding over them; we'll have to go down to that school and get some details on the spot. I was rather struck by Sweet's timing you know, he had twenty-five pounds down as being due before July 31st; I wonder if the threat was to advertise the facts, whatever they were, at the Southeys' party?"

"'Tis more than likely. But if one o' them bumped him off I wonder why they didna' take the notes back?"

"Too risky, Mac. Whoever was wandering round that morning with a fatal dose of sodium amytal isn't likely to have had time to rifle Sweet's pocket book. And of course there's nothing suspicious in a chap being found with twenty pounds in his wallet, it probably wouldn't occur to them that we'd trace the numbers of the notes and find the source of the money."

"Aye, that's right enough." The Scotsman nodded and put his foot down as the shining ribbon of empty road wound away ahead of them. The sun was spilling across the landscape now and the first warmth of day invaded the chill of dawn.

"That funny-looking stuff over there," remarked the sergeant, waving a hand at the close-turfed ramparts, long flattened and rounded by the weight of century on century, "that was something to do with these stone-age fellows, was it no'?"

"Hmm. They were the villages of the early Britons. In fact they were still living in villages protected by earth ramparts when the Romans came." He smiled at Mac's critical appraisal of the flattened humps as a means of defence. "That's what's left after a thousand years of weather," he laughed. "They probably weren't a bad defence against the sort of thing they were built for, though I expect the Romans found them a bit primitive. But the Ancient Britons were defeated more by indiscipline than inadequate defences, they were savage and courageous, but the legionaries were an organised army."

"We threw 'em out o' Scotland," retorted McGregor with a grin.

"Oh, yes, only the English could civilise the Scots!"

The road was still their own, and in the fields the larks stretched their small lungs with singing; in the distance rooks in the tall trees kept up their harsh running commentaries on the new day, and down among the stalks of the standing crops, small creatures busied themselves with the urgent matters of immediate nourishment and some harvesting towards the cold months ahead. A few rabbits, not yet deaf and blind with myxomatosis, nibbled the grass at the field's borders, and an occasional hare loped its way along a rutted path. The villages began to stir as they drew out of Wiltshire into Somerset, hens clucked and called in their varied and spasmodic chorus, there was a clanking of pails, an occasional child's shout, a morning greeting between two curling-pinned, clean-aproned housewives, already engaged on the day's work; the gruff comfortable voices of cowmen off to start the milking, and the barking of dogs. Day had already begun. The road carried them out of the village and the patchwork, hedged fields began again. The earth was clothed with crops; sturdy, heavy-eared wheat turning from green-gold to red-gold; is it history that makes this such a particularly satisfying crop Grainger wondered? They drove past the daintier, greener oats, a tangle of whiskers and hanging grains, past the dark fields of clover for winter feed; all a weighty component of the summer smells we love.

Paul Grainger and Rob McGregor, though the reason for their journey to a lunatic asylum lay in the activities of a murderer and a blackmailer in London, nevertheless felt caught up in the older, wider rhythm of approaching harvest-time. Although our lives may lie in the paved streets of cities and our preoccupations are with the involved activities of townsmen, it is this dark crust of earth that maintains all life on our planet, Grainger reminded himself. He was country-bred and whenever he left London, felt the pull of this older, slower way of life.

With something of an effort, he pulled his mind back to his case; it was going to be very difficult to get convincing circumstantial evidence about the method of administering the poison. As the case now stood William Southey had both the strongest motive and the best opportunity; he might be pressed to arrest the painter unless he could turn up some new evidence. Well, if he had done it he would have to pay for it, Grainger thought; but doubt nagged at him. Was it a personal liking for Southey, or was it a surer instinct for the truth? There was his wife, too. Southey was so much head of his household that there was a danger of casting her in too minor a role. Under her gentleness of manner there might well lie an inflexible will, and who could say to what lengths she might not go to protect her Catholic children from the knowledge that they were all bastards? On the other hand, if the real murderer lay elsewhere, the Southeys were proving a perfect cover for him. He shifted uneasily on his seat, this was proving the devil of a case.

A long-nosed car pulled out round them and slid down the road at a dangerous speed. To Grainger's surprise McGregor put his foot down on the accelerator and the police car raced after it.

"What is it, Mac, someone we know?"

"I canna' say for certain," replied the Scotsman, hugging the wheel as they swung round a bend that wasn't designed for speed, "he was goin' such a lick that I couldna' catch more than a glimpse, but it was a fellow with a beard, and there's no' so many o' those; and that car he's driving, that's an Alvis and there's no' so many o' those either. Wish I'd Southey's number with us now, but I havena', more's the pity." They roared up a hill as the Alvis disappeared over its crest. "He canna' keep this up all the way, we've towns to go through yet, supposin' he's bound for our destination. Sakes but he's got an engine in that bus!" he exclaimed as they topped a hill to see the other car disappearing round a distant bend.

"Well, it'll eat petrol," remarked Grainger. "If he's going as far as we are, he'll have to stop some time and fill up. What worries me rather more is that going at this pace he's likely to guess we're on his tail and I'd like to know what he's up to without being seen, so keep out of sight all you can, Mac. Oh, there he is again," the Superintendent exclaimed. "You've caught up a bit."

"Aye, 'tis the village had slowed him up. Trouble is it'll slow us up, too. Where'll be the first lot o' traffic lights now, I wonder?"

"Honiton, I think, I'm not sure, though. There'll be plenty in Exeter, of course, if he doesn't by-pass it. I wonder what he's after, if it is Southey?" He chewed the stem of his pipe reflectively: "Well, it'll be interesting to find out."

"If it's not a wild-goose chase I'm treating you to! If we do get a proper look at him the odds are it'll be a navy mon on his way to Plymouth."

"Well, we shall see," returned Grainger equably. "He's going to get us there early at least," he added, glancing at his watch.

"Aye, there's that to it." The sergeant cast a quick glance at the petrol gauge as the police car tore its way along the narrow road through Devonshire's fertile combes and wooded hills. "We'll be needing juice ourselves by the time we make Exeter," he said. But the Alvis stopped to fill up at Wimple and the police car drove past and identified the painter without difficulty, afterwards turning down a side road until they inconspicuously got on its tail again.

As they had conjectured, the painter led them to the asylum. Here, hidden from view they watched him get out of his car looking pale and tense. He stood for a moment looking up at the windows, and then disappeared inside. Nearly half an hour passed before he emerged again, and so different was his aspect that it was scarcely credible that he was the same man; he fitted his long body into the car in a leisurely fashion and sat there filling his pipe. He lit it and sat on, puffing and looking up at the building his face inscrutable, before he finally started his engine, turned his car and drove back along the road whence he had come.

"Hmm," remarked Grainger. "Probably he'll drive straight back to town, but we'll have him followed just in case. Go on to the local station, Mac, and fix it up with them, pick me up here when you've done."

"Aye, sir." Mac gave the asylum a hard look. "Give me the shivers those places," he remarked.

"Lunacy's a grim business," Grainger agreed.

Thornton, the asylum Superintendent was a middle-aged man of some weight, both corporal and spiritual, with a shock of wiry hair and shrewd blue eyes under prominent bushy eyebrows.

"Ah, Superintendent; I got your letter. Very glad to help you if I can." He shook hands with an iron grip and escorted Grainger into his room.

"About Mrs. Margaret Southey, isn't it? I have her file here. Curiously enough, we've already had an inquiry about her this morning. Her brother, nice fellow, hadn't seen him before, but I wasn't here when Mrs. Southey was admitted; that's quite a while ago, hmm, let me see now, yes here it is, 1928, twenty-seven years ago, she was only twenty at the time. A sad case, dementia praecox you know, you've probably heard it called schizophrenia; the Press talks a lot of rot about split personalities. They'd get a shock if they saw some of 'em. We've a good many of them here. Most of them come in young, plenty of them are women. We can do something for some of them, surgery you know, prefrontal leucotomy, you may have read about it, but by and large the prognosis is pretty bad. Dreadful disease, don't like it, rather have a melancholic or a senile dementia any day. Much more likeable, you know. Of course, at the time Mrs. Southey was admitted there was nothing you could do except to stop them hurting themselves and other people. Particularly other people. They're violent and dangerous. This woman"—he tapped the file—"was trying to murder her husband when she was certified. I've never seen him. Had to advertise for him when she was dying, but there was no response. One or two of our nurses have been here that long and they tell me he visited her regularly at first, but she deteriorated very rapidly and I suppose he gave it up as a bad job. Don't blame him. Shock to a normal person to see them in that state. Probably spent the rest of his life trying to forget it. But you didn't come here to listen to me gassing; fire away and I'll answer your questions as best I can."

Grainger smiled, "You've answered a lot of them already, sir. The only information I had was that Margaret Southey died here. I particularly wanted to know whether she had been an inmate, but that you have already told me. I'm rather interested that her brother should have inquired after her today, quite a coincidence. Did he give any reason, I wonder, for looking her up at this late date?"

"Oh yes, he said he'd been abroad for a number of years, and knowing she was admitted here before he went, he thought he'd come down and see if she was still here and how she was doing. He didn't know she was dead. Seemed rather relieved to hear it, more than he let on, I thought privately. Of course, relations of that sort are an embarrassment."

"You gathered, then, that he had not visited her for many years?"

"Not since she was first admitted. I couldn't give him much comfort, poor chap, except that she was dead at last. She'd been in a bad way ever since I've been here. Shocking heredity, her mother's in Broadmoor, still living I believe. She murdered the father when Margaret was only ten. The child found him."

Grainger shook his head. "It's horrifying," he said, "I thought we police officers saw the seamy side, but it's cakes and ale compared with your lot."

Thornton laughed. "Oh, you get used to it. And it has its interest, especially the more curable cases. There are lots of 'em that settle down very happily in the asylum, too, you know. They wouldn't make out if they were out in the rough and tumble of everyday life, but they settle down to a world of their own in here and are surprisingly contented. Live into the eighties often. Of course the oddest things may upset them. We had rather an amusing example the other day, trying out the results of vitamin tablets. They can be useful in lunacy in large enough doses. We selected a ward, issued tablets to half of it, kept the other half without as control. Result—a free fight! The tablet half were convinced we were trying to poison them, the other half were furious at missing something good!"

Grainger laughed. "It's a good thing everything has its amusing side," he remarked. "About Mrs. Southey's brother—what was his name?"

"Howard."

"Oh yes, Mr. Howard. Did he see any of the staff who were here when he last visited his sister?"

"No. I did ask him if he would like to talk to one of the nurses who was in charge of her, but he said no, since she was dead and there was nothing he could do for her, he wouldn't waste anyone's time. As I mentioned he seemed rather relieved that the whole sorry business was over, no joke having half your family in lunatic asylums. Though if people did but realise it, madness is much more common than the man in the street could dream of. If you included all the people who are walking about, but very far from what we call normal, the proportion of unbalanced to balanced would be so high that it would frighten you."

"Is that so? Is it increasing, do you think?"

"It's easy to get that impression, but not so simple to give a reliable opinion. As society gets more tightly organised these people show up more, y'see. You think of those big Victorian families, I wonder how many of their eccentric aunts would be labelled mad, or at least seriously neurotic now? It's a bit like the cancer figures, they seem to increase, but I wonder how many died in the past and were buried under different labels because it wasn't picked up?"

"Figures can be deceiving." Grainger refilled his pipe thoughtfully. "Did Mrs. Southey ever mention her husband to you?"

"She would speak at times of someone she called Jack. But her conversation, if you can call it such, was very disconnected. Like many schizophrenics, she showed paranoid tendencies and accused innumerable people of being responsible for her predicament. Would you like to speak to one of the nurses who used to attend to her?"

"Thank you, sir, I should. Actually I'd particularly like to see any nurse who might remember her husband."

"Her husband, eh, he's turned up again has he?" He looked up as if about to ask a question and then changed his mind and grinned at the police officer. "Well, you won't want to be bothered with my curiosity. Nurse Daniels has been here for some thirty years and she may be able to help you." He touched a bell on his desk and a pretty young Cornish girl with thick hair as black as a kitten's came in from an adjoining room.

"Could you ask Nurse Daniels to come here for a moment, Miss Williams?"

"Nice girl, isn't she?" remarked Thornton when she had departed on her errand. "She came as a patient and stayed as my secretary."

Grainger looked surprised, "She doesn't mind staying on at the asylum?"

"She loves it here. She hadn't a home fit to return to. I was anxious she wouldn't have to go back there as a matter of fact. She takes a great interest in the patients and it's good for them to see somebody about who's cleared the fence, so to speak. Especially the milder cases. Though it makes for a lot of jealousy as well. A doctor in an asylum is much more involved in the emotional life of his patients than is strictly comfortable." He laughed. "But Miss Williams is a great success; she's just got engaged to one of my young assistants. The whole place is buzzing with it."

Nurse Daniels was a thick-set woman with an imperturbable face and a pair of patient brown eyes set deep in wrinkles.

"I won't keep you long, Sister," remarked Grainger, smiling at her, "I expect you're very busy?"

"Oh yez, sir, we'm alwayz buzy here."

"Dr. Thornton tells me you have been here for more than thirty years and I am hoping you may be able to help me, for that means you were here when Mrs. Margaret Southey was admitted. Do you remember the occasion at all?"

"Oh, yez, zir, I do mind that ever zo well. 'Twere in middle o' night she did come 'ere, ravin' and violent she waz, wantin' to kill her husband. Zeemz they juzt stopped her when she got 'er 'ands on 'iz windpipe and she waz that mad about it, we 'ad to put 'er in padded cell."

"It's a great help to find you have such a good memory, Sister. Can you tell me whether her husband was with her that night?"

"Oh, yez, zir, Mr. Southey were there, poor mun, I do remember 'un, that pale and upzet like, and who's to wonder at it. Ordinary folk don't be used to their goings on like what we are. Only a young fellow 'e waz and married juzt a few months. We waz zorry for 'un like."

"Did you see him again after that night?"

"Oh yez, zir, 'e came to vizit 'er reg'lar at firzt 'e did, but it were no good az I could ha' told 'un. If so be she was quiet afore 'e come, it waz alwayz the zame az zoon az she zet eyes on 'un. Straight for 'is throat often as not. Or if so be it weren't that, she'd yell at 'un all the dirty rubbish in 'er poor mind, zur, it's juzt the way they go on like."

"Do you think you could give me a description of Mr. Southey after all these years, Sister?"

"Well, zur, I can do my best, zur, though I'm not much 'and at zuch things." She paused a moment and Grainger could see her faithfully scrutinising her memory.

"'E were a tall young fellow," she began, "and nicely zet up. 'E'd a lot o' brown hair that fell over his forehead like. I think maybe 'e was forgetful about going to barber, 'e was one o' they artists from St. Ives and 'e dressed funny." She looked appealingly at Grainger, "Maybe you know what I mean, zur, I've heard tell as you do 'ave a lot o' they in London, 'e did talk like folks from London, begging your pardon, zur."

"That's most helpful, Sister," smiled Grainger. "Can you tell me whether he wore a beard?"

"Oh, no, zur. 'E didn't have no beard, just 'iz 'air rather long and one o' they funny-coloured shirts with no tie and a zuit o' fuztianz. 'E brought 'er a picture once, zaid it might be homely for 'er to have on wall by 'er bed like, but she took and tore it into shreds."

"Did Mrs. Southey talk about him much to you?"

"Well, zur, when she was took like that she'd shoot out a lot o' dirty things about 'un o' course, but we'm uzed to that and we don't take no more notice than if it waz thundering like. Zometimes it would be 'im she waz getting at, and then again it might be me or Doctor, or one o' the others. She thought we waz all in it together to keep her locked up. She'd zay we waz afraid to let her out because of all the bad thingz she did know about uz. But lots of them do that, zur, it don't mean nothing."

"I quite understand, Sister. Do you remember when Mr. Southey stopped visiting his wife?"

"Well I couldn't zay for zertain zure, zur, but I think az it waz in the winter after she did come here."

"And she came at what time of year?"

Thornton looked up from his file. "March," he said briefly.

"And you've never seen Mr. Southey since that time?" Sister Daniel hesitated a moment and then said a little uncertainly, "No, zur."

Grainger smiled at her encouragingly, "You hesitated, Sister, did you wonder perhaps if you might have seen him again, but not feel sure enough to mention it?"

"Well, it's funny as you should zay that, zur. It were thiz morning. I were in Ward Two, and I just happened to look out o' window, it looks over front, that window does, and there was a man ztanding there, looking up at our windows and I thought to myself, do zeem 'e puts me in mind o' zomebody. But I couldn't bring to mind who it might be. Drezzed very smart 'e waz, a tall man with a beard and a great forehead, 'e weren't wearing no hat. But it weren't hizzelf if you underztand me, zur, it were the way he looked up at they windows, very zad like az if it broke hiz heart to think o' all our folkz inzide."

"And it occurs to you now that it might have been Mr. Southey?"

"Well now, zur, I couldn't zay a thing like that," replied the Sister with a hint of reproof. What a very honest and accurate witness, Grainger thought, watching the heavy wrinkled face. "But when you did ask me juzt then, it came to me that waz how Mr. Southey did uzed to look up at they windows."

Grainger was aware of Thornton's gaze fixed on his face in lively speculation. He smiled at Sister Daniel.

"Thank you, Sister. You have been very helpful indeed. I was most fortunate to find someone who had been here long enough to help me and possessing such an excellent memory."

Amazingly Sister Daniel blushed. "Very glad to be of azziztanze, zur," she said demurely. She turned inquiringly to Dr. Thornton.

"Yes, that's all, Sister, we won't keep you any longer from your patients. I don't know what they'll be getting up to without you!"

Sister took herself out with a bustle of starched skirts.

Thornton laughed. "You've made her day, Superintendent, more insults than compliments come her way, poor faithful soul. She's a damn good Sister, mind you, but the patients can be quite abominably rude to them, you know, and they get a sort of instinct for hitting where it hurts most. Heaven knows it's difficult enough to get good nurses, but what amazes me is that we get any. As you know they're ridiculously underpaid, and this job's both dirty and tough." He stopped speaking and eyed the police officer quizzically, "Well, I gather you've got some of the information you want anyway?" he offered. Grainger smiled and shook his head as he said:

"I'm afraid it must be most tantalising for you. I'm sorry I can't tell you more about it; but it might be unfair to some of the parties involved."

"Of course, of course," responded Thornton quickly. "Living out here in the wilds, we rather lap up any intrusion from London you know." He rose. "Well, I hope we've helped you along a bit, I shall watch the papers for your case."

Grainger left him a few minutes later, standing rather forlornly on the steps of the big stone building.

"So they let you out, did they?" Mac greeted him.

"This time," his chief smiled back. "Off we go. I'll tell you about it on the way."

# FOURTEEN

Henry Meade sat on an upturned box, his tubular trunk thrust forward between his bent knees, his long face stiff with controlled anxiety, the thin lips a straight line under his small moustache, a big forked vein standing out in his forehead. Beside him, a pile of wilting weeds bore evidence to the ferocious energy with which he was attacking his herbaceous border; overhead, the August sun poured mercilessly down. Far away in Cornwall, Superintendent Grainger was talking to Dr. Thornton about mad Mrs. Southey and her husband; in the near-by cemetery, Ivan Sweet lay in his grave and already the cells of his dead body had turned to their own destruction, liquefying the solid flesh in advance of the putrefying bacteria and the grosser worms. In her elegant bedroom on the first floor of Henry Meade's cottage, twisting and turning with pain, her mind reeling with fear, lay the girl who had loved that thing that was now Ivan Sweet...

Her father worked on with cold deliberation, determined not to panic about his daughter's condition. He had set himself to weed a certain sector of the bed before he allowed himself to go to her again and make the difficult decision about calling in outside help.

He heard her groan as he climbed the stairs and quickened his steps with a beating heart. But she was quiet when he entered the room, looking up at him with terror, her small even teeth fastened

on a pallid lip. Panic and anger shook him but he kept them out
of his voice as he said:

"I'm going to fetch Dr. Shepherd, love."

But she became so hysterical at the suggestion that in the end
he telephoned Caroline Southey.

She, too, was working hard to still the apprehensions that
clamoured for her attention. She was taking advantage of William's
absence in Cornwall to give his crowded studio a thorough turn-
out. She rather enjoyed the job as a rule, but today... today she
would work hard for a little only to find herself standing still with
some object forgotten in her hand, while her mind worried at the
problems that obsessed it and despaired at the impossibility of every
imagined solution. The telephone shrilling at her elbow startled her
so much that she dropped the picture she was holding. It was an
early one of Elaine at three, round-limbed and grave-faced. With
trembling hands she picked it up and her heart cold with fear, laid
it gently on the desk before she answered the phone. She held it
unwillingly to her ear, forgetting to say Hullo, and for a moment
failed to recognise the voice repeating an agitated Hullo, Hullo!

"Hullo," she answered at last.

"Oh, Caroline, I'm so glad you are in"—belatedly she recognised Henry Meade's voice. "I find myself very much worried, I
hope you will forgive me for troubling you with it, but I would
be so grateful if you could spare a moment to come up here. I
wouldn't ask but that I am very anxious. Yolande has been taken
ill, she's in great pain and—very distressed. She is quite unwilling
to see our doctor... I know it's rather much to ask, but I feel a
sympathetic woman friend..."

"But of course I'll come, Henry; I'll be with you in five
minutes."

Caroline hurried along the street and turned in at the Meades' gate. It was a relief to turn her attention to someone else's troubles and she felt rather more in command of herself. Henry was waiting for her and took her straight up to Yolande. It took her only a few moments to realise that the girl was in urgent need of medical attention, and after calming the child as best she could, she ran down to the anxious old man and told him to ring the doctor without delay and to warn him that the girl might need to go into hospital.

Upstairs she found Yolande completely preoccupied with pain and weakening visibly under the loss of blood. When she had done what little she could for her comfort, the older woman sat beside her while the minutes ticked away till help should arrive. She tried to pray, but her mind twisted away from the familiar words so that they lost all meaning; can't I even pray for this poor child's sake, she thought in despair. The grim nightmare that had settled on their own lives since Ivan Sweet's death seemed to have gripped this household, too... the hated name started another train of thought; Ivan Sweet, of course. She stared compassionately at the averted face of the girl on the bed, this was yet another tragedy for which he was responsible... the swine, she thought, my God the filthy swine!

Two pairs of feet on the stairs at last announced the doctor's coming. He examined the girl and gave Caroline an appraising glance.

"I'm going to ring for an ambulance," he said quietly. "Come and tell me at once if there's any change, will you?"

Caroline nodded and returning to her chair by Yolande's bedside, took the white flaccid hand in her own again. The girl was very quiet now and her mind wandered for a moment to William in Cornwall… What news would he bring back… and what could they do…? A slight sound from the bed brought her thoughts back with a rush and she stood up and bent over the girl. Why was she so still? Caroline was appalled at her almost transparent pallor; she leant closer, had there been a change? A cold fear gripped her and she was caught in an agony of indecision, then just as she had decided to race for the doctor, Yolande opened her eyes and stared straight up into her face.

"Am I going to die?" she asked.

"No, of course you're not." Caroline knelt down and slipped an arm round the girl's shoulders.

"We're going to take you into hospital to stop this bleeding and they'll give you a transfusion to make up for all you've lost. Don't worry, darling, just leave it all to us."

"Will it stop hurting soon? It hurts an awful lot."

"I know, darling. But they'll give you something so that you won't feel it so much." Yolande nodded. After a moment she said:

"Caroline?"

"Yes, darling?"

"I think, before this I was going to have a baby… it won't come now, will it?"

"No. Almost certainly not."

"Promise me you won't tell Daddy?"

"Of course I won't. Don't worry about all that now. Everything will come right in time, I promise you."

"Do you think so?"

"I know."

Yolande was silent. After a little she said, "You see it was Ivan's baby. Daddy… hated him."

"Yes, darling." Caroline found herself fighting her own battle; it was horribly difficult to force down a sense of relief at finding someone else with a motive for killing Ivan Sweet.

"Do you think Daddy knows?"

Caroline hesitated, "He may, but that won't stop him from loving you and wanting to do everything in the world to make life good for you again." She smiled soberly at the sick girl, "Perhaps it sounds heartless now, but one day you'll only remember the nice bits of all this time."

A great sobbing sigh escaped the girl, breaking her voice as she cried, "It was nice in the beginning... oh, Caroline, it was wonderful... and I couldn't tell anyone because he and Daddy hated each other always."

"Yes." Caroline smiled sadly as she stroked the hair back from the clammy forehead.

"But it hasn't been nice... for quite long... Ivan was going to marry me... but, sometimes I wondered... oh I don't know... and then someone killed him and there was the baby and I didn't know what to do and I couldn't tell anyone... and I've been so frightened!" she sobbed.

"Of course you have, you've been a very brave girl..." To her relief Caroline heard footsteps mounting the stairs. She gripped the childish hand and whispered, "I'll come with you in the ambulance."

Yolande, to her surprise, felt less frightened when at last she was in hospital. Everyone was calm and confident and the pain wasn't so unbearable. There had been tablets to take and injections and everything was more matter of fact and the cold shaking of fear was getting less. She began to grow sleepy, the room was getting blurred...

As soon as Yolande lost consciousness, Caroline left. She found Henry sitting bolt upright in the waiting-room, his face set rigidly, his trembling hands clasped together. He hardly seemed to hear her attempts at comfort, but just nodded his head jerkily.

When she got home it was to find that William had phoned, but there was no message except that he was on his way home. Wearily she climbed the stairs to the room they shared. Downstairs the front door banged. She hurried to the head of the stairs to look down, although it wasn't reasonable that William could be back yet. No it wasn't William. It was Elaine, and how miserable she looked! What could have happened between her and Jonathon the other day? It seemed to Caroline as if within her the last barricade against her hopelessness collapsed. Feeling incapable of comforting anyone, even Elaine, she crept back to her room and sat on the window-seat, her head in her hands.

Out in the garden the baby started to cry. Mrs. Lion stopped her kitchen clatter to listen; his mother or one of his sisters always went to the baby when he cried. But he went on crying. Shaking her head Mrs. Lion dried her hands and went out to fetch him. Outside the sky was high and blue and the sun's heat distilled the scent of multitudinous flowers, but loyal Mrs. Lion was not to be mollified. Her old down-at-heel sandals clattered down the stone path as she hurried to the pram; the little boy was screaming now, hungry and unaccustomed to such neglect. Mrs. Lion broke into a shambling run, her kindly bird-like face poking forward on her long discoloured neck, her unsuitably low-cut summer dress slipping off one bony, work-bowed shoulder. Her brightly painted lips moved over her carious teeth, "I'll give Mr. Sweet murder, drat 'im!" she muttered. She reached the pram and bent over it, her angular face dissolving in tenderness as she spoke to the indignant little boy. Her red, knobbly-knuckled hands were gentle as she lifted him and carried him in to his sadly disorganised home.

# FIFTEEN

E ARLY NEXT MORNING, GRAINGER PUSHED OPEN THE HEAVY
street door of Magnolia House and walked thoughtfully
down the cloister. Reaching the end, he suddenly stopped and
stared intently at the six neat pigeon-holes arranged in pairs and
attached to the wall of the house. He read the order cards slotted
into the backs of the wooden boxes. What a blind fool I am, he
thought, nothing could be simpler. He turned and looked down
the cloister; no windows overlooked it; pushing aside the hanging
creeper he leant through one of the arches to look at the garage
drive beyond; yes the gates would be just out of view of the
windows of the house.

"Daddy's in his studio," Elaine stated when he asked for
Southey. "Do you know the way?"

The painter was standing at the window when the detective entered. "Please sit down, Superintendent," he said. "I had
expected that we would see you again soon." He sat down himself
in silence, waiting for the policeman to speak.

"Have you any idea why I have come today?" Grainger asked
after a moment. Southey regarded him steadily.

"Obviously there could be any number of reasons,
Superintendent," he replied, "but possibly I understand you. I
will answer any questions you may care to ask."

Paul Grainger's eyes held the painter's for a few moments
in silence, then raising his chin and blinking his sandy lashes,

he said, "You didn't tell me that Ivan Sweet was blackmailing you."

Southey nodded slowly.

"No, I didn't tell you," he answered. "I was aware of course that I should have done. Also I was very loath to do so. You will understand I think that one shrinks from volunteering information of this sort. I realised of course that the time would almost certainly come when you would ask me about it, but"—he shrugged—"I suppose it is a human weakness to hope that such eventualities may not materialise."

"Where a man has been killed, such information is very relevant."

"Oh, yes, I realise my position only too well. Nevertheless for what it's worth, although as a result of my own misdoing he had me in his power, I did not kill Ivan Sweet. It is of course useless to deny, however, that I am glad he is dead."

"You refer to 'your own misdoing'. I have to ask you to explain that phrase."

The painter regarded him with a faint smile.

"I have no doubt that you are now as well informed as I am myself on the subject of my unsavoury past, Superintendent, but I am in no position to object to the necessary form. Briefly then, I am a bigamist and my children are illegitimate. My first—I should say—my wife," he grimaced, "died last year in an asylum in Cornwall where she had been an inmate for twenty-seven years."

"How did Mr. Sweet come by this knowledge?"

"I wish I knew. Trying to answer that question was quite an obsession with me at one time. I have never taken anyone into my confidence in this matter and how he could have found out was a complete mystery to me."

"How long had Sweet been blackmailing you?"

"Since last November. He came in one night when I was work-ing alone in here and asked me to lend him five hundred pounds. I told him not to be ridiculous. He spun some tale about what he wanted it for, but I was working and didn't listen. Finally I told him to get out. He became abusive and told me I would regret it; I replied that that was my affair. He fixed me with those cold eyes of his, like a snake about to strike, and said perhaps it was my wife's affair, too. I was furious and he went on, 'It was inaccurate of me to say your wife, I should have said your kept woman. How will you like it when I tell her that your brats are bastards?'"

Grainger frowned, "Perhaps it's improper of me to say so, Mr. Southey, but you might like to know that no one loathes blackmailers more than we do in the police force." He sucked at his pipe and asked, "What happened next?"

Southey gave him a rather grim smile. "I appreciate your remark, Superintendent, I won't try to excuse what I did in mar-rying when I was not free to do so, events have proved that I was wrong. There is nothing to say except that I am glad that now the divorce laws have at last been amended, no one need find himself in the position in which I found myself twenty-two years ago. You ask me what happened next. I was, of course, indescribably shocked. If I had killed Sweet, it would have been then, when I saw that he held the happiness and dignity of my wife and all my children in his filthy hands. I will admit the temptation came to me then. But the moment passed. I collected my wits as best I could and tried to make my mind function to save what was possible from the wreck. It wasn't easy but something had to be done. It was the more difficult in that I couldn't imagine the source of his information. I'm afraid I had for years acted the ostrich about my first wife; as you will have gathered, she was a homicidal lunatic and she represented a chapter in my life that I was unable to remember without horror. Now, I thought, if Sweet knew, perhaps others knew, too, I could not gauge the extent of my danger. Finally I told him that I would pay him forty pounds every month in cash but that if he made any attempt to increase this amount I would charge him with blackmail and take the consequences. I estimated that with a safe five hundred pounds a year coming in from me he wouldn't risk losing it. I think he believed me when I said I'd turn him over to the police, and indeed I meant it."

"It is a very great pity you didn't turn him over to us immediately, Mr. Southey. Perhaps you were unaware that we guarantee anonymity to victims of a blackmail case and that we very rarely prosecute for the original cause of the blackmail. It is a great pity that more people don't realise how discreet the police are in such cases as yours."

Southey was staring at him with a frown. "No. I didn't realise that," he answered slowly.

"Did Sweet in fact make any further demands?"

"No. I paid him forty pounds on the first of each month. Needless to say, it was a great financial strain and I had to face the fact that it was going to be difficult to educate my younger children, but it was the lesser evil. I reminded him of my conditions on each occasion—he was very surly but made no attempt to alter them."

"And you believed your—your wife to be quite ignorant of all this?"

"Had she not been ignorant of it, it is doubtful whether I would have allowed myself to be blackmailed, Superintendent."

"I see. I wonder whether it would be possible for her to come in here for a few moments?"

The painter's unease for once showed in his face, but he answered equably enough, "Yes, of course. I'll go and find her."

He was gone some time and when he returned with Caroline he looked more distressed than Grainger had yet seen him. She smiled at him distractedly and began to speak rapidly.

"Superintendent Grainger, I must tell you at once that I know about William's marriage to that poor mad woman in Cornwall. Mr. Sweet was blackmailing me about it, he threatened to tell my children that they are not legitimate. I know William has been trying to protect me in case you think I killed him, but I want you to know. I'm afraid I owe you an apology for not telling you before, but I will tell you all about it now; I paid him fifty pounds out of my savings book in April, and he asked me for another fifty pounds last month but I told him that I couldn't manage it until I'd sold some jewellery. He pretended to be very considerate, rather laughably in the circumstances I thought, and told me not to do that for his sake. He would wait he said until I could afford it without that."

Southey laughed grimly, "No wonder he was 'so considerate', he knew very well that if I'd found out he was blackmailing you, too, I'd have turned him over to the police."

"I know, darling, I ought to have told you in the beginning..." said Caroline.

"Caro, sweet, don't start talking about what *you* should have told *me!* It's what I should have told you." The painter shook his head helplessly as he spoke.

"Thank you, Mrs. Southey," Grainger said. "You've answered the questions I wanted to ask you." He paused. "There's a small practical point I wanted to inquire about; the tradesmen's pigeon-holes you have on the wall outside. Am I right in thinking that there are two for each household?"

"Oh yes, that's quite right, Superintendent. Everyone fills in their needs on the cards provided and the milkman and the baker simply put the goods ordered in the boxes."

"Can you tell me at what times the tradesmen call?"

"Oh yes, it varies of course according to the day of the week..."

"If you could tell me the usual times on a Saturday, that would be sufficient."

"Saturday, yes, well the milkman usually comes before nine o'clock, say about ten to as a rule, and the baker about eleven-thirty."

"And can you give me any idea of the time when Mrs. Moore and Mr. Sweet collected their goods from the pigeon-holes last Saturday?"

"Well, Superintendent, last Saturday we were all rather busy with the party, but I'll tell you as far as I can remember, and you could ask Mrs. Lion and Mrs. Moore as well. I remember I sent Christine out to collect our milk and things as soon as the milkman came. I rather think Mrs. Moore came down soon afterwards, about twenty past nine perhaps. I didn't see Mr. Sweet myself that morning."

"Can you give me any idea of the time at which he would usually collect his goods on a Saturday?"

"Oh probably about eleven or twelve. Even later sometimes, his box was always the last to be emptied."

"Did he have a regular order?"

"Well, he had half a pint of milk and a small carton of cream every day, and butter and eggs from time to time."

"You didn't notice anything unusual on that morning, I mean, you didn't notice later that the goods in his pigeon-hole hadn't been collected, or any detail of that sort?"

Caroline frowned, "I'm afraid I haven't any conscious memory, Superintendent."

"You didn't notice anything?" Grainger asked, turning to the painter.

William shook his head.

At Grainger's request they descended to the kitchen and tackled Mrs. Lion.

"Aow. What does 'e want ter know that for?" inquired that good woman suspiciously. Caroline looked helplessly at Grainger who smiled pacifically and answered:

"All sorts of little details help us when we're solving a crime, Mrs. Lion, we have to ask lots of people what seem to them very silly questions. Our job is to find the murderer so that he can be punished and all the innocent people mixed up in the case can be cleared of suspicion. I'm sure you will want to help us do that."

Mrs. Lion glanced at Caroline who smiled encouragingly at her. "Aow well, prob'ly won't do no 'arm to tell yer," she conceded reluctantly. She considered a moment, looking up at the kitchen clock on the wall to help her memory.

"Mrs. Moore came down first as per usual, 'bout quarter past nine that would 'a' bin. She were all dressed up, she were goin' down West that mornin' so she tol' me Friday. Mr. Sweet"—she spat the name out—"'e come up in 'is 'ighly coloured dressin'-gown when all decent folks 'ad 'ad their brekfas's and washed 'em up long ago. Ten past eleven that wos by this clock 'ere."

"Thank you, Mrs. Lion, that's most helpful. Now I wonder if you can tell me what Mr. Sweet's order to the milkman was that day?"

"Aow, 'e always 'ad the sime, 'alf a pint o' milk and a carton o' cream fer 'is corfee."

"And he collected both these when he came up, did he?"

Mrs. Lion gave him a pitying look, "'Course 'e did, 'e wasn't one to give 'iself trouble."

"The milkman had already been when you arrived, had he?"

"Tha's right. 'E's always bin time I come. I can't git 'ere before nine, see."

"You didn't see anyone near the pigeon-holes when you came?"

"Aow naow, there weren't nobody abart then."

"And later, did you notice anyone hanging about those pigeon-holes at any time?"

"See 'ere, mister, I can't see them boxes through a brick wall. I knew when Mrs. Moore brought hers in 'cos I was in me kitchen with the door open and I could see her through the 'all, and when Mr. Sweet come up for 'is I wos comin' downstairs after doin' bedrooms. If yer wants ter know, I did see some folks wot come to Miss Elaine's party that night, out o' me kitchen winder that mornin', but if I said I sor 'em muckin' abart wiv them there pigin-'oles, it'ud be a fib, see?"

"Yes, I quite understand, no one appreciates accuracy more than we do, Mrs. Lion, you are an excellent witness. You say you saw several of the party guests that morning, did you happen to know their names?"

"Well, there was Mr. Meade, I knowed 'im o' course, but I don't rightly know 'oo the other two was, though I saw 'em ag'in that night. I come along ter give Mrs. Southey a 'and wiv the glasses."

"Could you describe these people do you think?"

"Reckon I could if I give me mind to it," Mrs. Lion frowned with painful concentration. "The first one, 'e was a little chap with them funny glasses wot pinch the top o' your nose."

"I should think that would be Cecil Paignton," said Caroline a little uncomfortably, "but I didn't see him myself."

"And the other one?"

"'E was a thin dark chap, kind a' nervy looking. 'E needed to 'ave patches sewed on the elbows of 'is jacket. 'E did put me in mind o' someone, but I ain't sure 'oo it met be."

"He didn't remind you of Mr. Sweet by any chance?"

Mrs. Lion gazed at the detective with admiration.

"Well, I call that real clever! Yep. That's 'oo 'e reminded me of. Not that 'e was that like, you know, just 'ad a sort o' look of 'im if yer knows wot I mean."

Grainger turned to Caroline, "Did you notice Mr. Patrick Sweet that morning? I suppose he didn't call?"

She shook her head, "No. And I certainly didn't notice him. How extraordinary, I wonder what he was doing?"

"'E was jist wanderin' round the 'ouse like as if 'e 'ad something on 'is mind. I only noticed 'im 'cos 'e seemed ter keep goin' away and comin' back agin, and I wondered wot 'e could be up to, 'e wos be'aving so funny like. Come to think of it," she added, warming to her task, "I saw that Mrs. Jonas 'anging around, too, but that's nuffin' new o' course, she or that spiteful girl o' 'ers is always spyin' on us in this 'ouse."

"You mentioned you saw Mr. Meade; did he call here perhaps?" Grainger asked, turning to Caroline.

"No. Though as a matter of fact I did notice him outside but he just hesitated a moment or two by the street door and walked on down the hill."

"About what time was this?"

"About half-past ten I think."

"'E must a' come back then," Mrs. Lion broke in, "'cos I seed 'im walking t'other way, up the 'ill, must 'a' bin goin' on fer eleven. Yep it were jist before Mr. Sweet come in wiv 'is milk and cream."

"Thank you, Mrs. Lion. I wonder if you can do as well with the others, did you happen to notice what time you saw Mrs. Jonas for instance?"

Mrs. Lion considered. "Naow," she said regretfully, "'fraid I can't. She's always 'angin' abart see, I wouldn't think nothin' special to it, I seed 'er lots o' mornin's and met git the times mixed up, see."

"I quite understand," assented Grainger. "How about the dark young man who looked rather like Mr. Sweet?"

"Well, it was jist after I saw Mr. Meade, that'd be near enough, wouldn't it?"

"Did you notice him hanging about for long?"

"Naow, but that's not to say 'e wasn't. 'E wos outside lookin' down at the basement winders when I went upstairs to do the bedrooms. It wos comin' daown agin arter that that I met Mr. Sweet comin' in wiv 'is milk and 'is cream. Time I got back to the kitchen, chap outside 'ad cleared orf. Quarter past eleven it was then."

"Thank you," Grainger was noting down the various times. "And the little plump gentleman, possibly Mr. Paignton, did you happen to notice the time when he was about?"

"Well, I couldn't say for Gospel, but 'e was early, I can tell you that. Soon arter I come, it wos, an' 'e looked that queer, that's wot made me look at 'im, lookin' at the 'ouse as if 'e didn't want ter but couldn't 'elp 'isself like. 'E got one o' them raound pasty faces, and yer couldn't see as 'e'd got eyes be'ind 'is glasses, the sun was shinin' on them like winders; 'e walked funny, like as if 'e wos ashamed of 'isself. Beggin' yer pardon, Mrs. Southey, if 'e was a friend o' yours, but 'e did give me the shivers and that's a fact."

"I know what you mean, Mrs. Lion, and he's only an acquaintance I've always felt rather sorry for," Caroline answered, rather embarrassed.

"Thank you very much. Now only one small point." Grainger continued to Mrs. Lion, "Do you know whether Mr. Sweet ordered any bread, and if so when it was collected? I think you said the baker comes about eleven, didn't you?" he added, turning to Caroline. She nodded, and Mrs. Lion said at once, "Oh yes, 'e 'ad a small 'Ovis, I see it there when I was sweeping that there passage and I brought it in fer 'im and took it daown wiv me when I went later ter do 'is bit o' cleaning."

"Thank you. That was just before one o'clock, wasn't it?"

"Thassrigh'," answered Mrs. Lion.

As Caroline was showing him out, Grainger turned to her and asked casually, "Have you a hypodermic syringe in the house, do you know, Mrs. Southey?"

Caroline looked astonished. "No, Superintendent, we've never possessed such a thing."

"Should you by any chance come across one, will you let me know at once?"

"Of course, Superintendent, but I think it most unlikely."

"You never know," smiled Grainger. "If you should come across one, don't handle it at all, just get in touch with me right away. Would you ask Mrs. Moore to look out for one, too, please?"

Caroline looked still more astonished, but agreed to do as he asked. "But surely," she added, as a thought occurred to her, "if there was one anywhere in the house, you and your sergeant would have found it in your search?"

Grainger smiled rather enigmatically, "I think it possible that one may turn up," he answered. And he was gone.

# SIXTEEN

"A FEW SECONDS WOULD HAVE SUFFICED FOR THE MUR-derer to inject a fatal dose into that carton of cream if he were armed with a hypodermic charged with poison; and if the needle were inserted at an angle through the intact lid, the prick wouldn't show to casual inspection."

McGregor nodded slowly as he listened to Grainger's speculations.

"Aye, 'tis neat, that. 'Twould account for a lot o' things if that was the way of it." He pulled out round a tractor while he thoughtfully considered his chief's suggestion of the *modus operandi* of this killing. There had been a time, he remembered sometimes with shame, when in the sergeants' mess-room he had poured scorn on Grainger's 'guessing'; well, he'd had to eat his own words, he thought now, smiling grimly at the long-ago memories; but now, though his chief would tell him how he arrived at one of his inspired guesses, some corner of his Scottish soul clung to the alluring belief that his super had second sight.

"Damn nuisance that carton was burnt," Grainger remarked regretfully; "I should like to have proved it short of a confession. Of course a hypodermic wouldn't be strictly necessary, the lid could have been prised up and replaced. Take longer though and it might look as though it had been tampered with." Grainger stretched his legs and drew reflectively at his pipe.

"It leaves us wi' a guid bunch of 'em could ha' done it, more's the pity! We'll be needin' a hundred per cent check on who was near that cloister place between eight-fifty when that cream was put there and eleven-ten when the dead man collected it. O' course," he continued, after a moment's reflection, "'twould have to be a body that knew the man took a whole carton of cream wi' his breakfas' coffee."

Grainger laughed, "Sweet's extravagance in that matter sticks in your gullet, doesn't it, Mac?"

"Aye, and he'd ha' been better off if it'd stuck in his!"

"Maybe you've got something there," remarked the other, "if he hadn't been greedy it's unlikely that he would have been murdered. It looks as though whoever killed him utilised one of his little greeds to put a final stop to the big one."

McGregor nodded as he stopped the car at a country crossroads and leant forward to read the signpost.

"Straight over," directed Grainger.

"Now we've rumoured it amang the lot o' them that we're expectin' to find one o' these hypodermic syringes we may get some jumps out o' them. Reckon someone may think the time right to do a bit o' plantin'. Should be interesting."

Grainger nodded. "It'll be interesting whichever way it goes. If our chaps pick up who's moving it'll be very interesting indeed, but it's a difficult watch to keep of course. The killer's best course would be to sit tight, especially if that was the method used, but every murderer must be an opportunist to some extent and I think we may tempt him out of his strategic immobility."

"Aye." McGregor put his foot down on the accelerator and the big car hummed powerfully as it climbed the winding wooded hill, dropping again to a quiet purr as it sped along a ridge of the Chiltern hills.

"Must be quite near here," he remarked. "'Tis a pleasant spot for a school."

"Hmm. It is, isn't it? I'll own I'm curious to know what Sweet had on the Jonas's. One or both parents must have taught there then I suppose, and possibly the child attended the school as well. Slow up a bit, Mac," he said suddenly, "I think it may be this next turning to the right... yes, it is, we should be there in a few minutes now."

"One o' these 'progressive' places, isn't it now?" McGregor made the adjective sound like an insult. "All play and no work."

"Oh, I expect they get a good bit done, though they probably have a different way of doing it," smiled Grainger. "Anyway you should approve of them, they're co-educational, like your Scottish schools. Ah, here's the gate, in we go. That must be the porter's lodge," he remarked as they passed a small building. "After you've dropped me, Mac, have a chat with the porter. If he's been here long enough to cover the period we're interested in, you might get more information out of him than I can get out of a stone-walling headmistress!"

Grainger had only to listen for a moment to know that the children were at break. He reached the main school building, a rather lovely country house that still wore an air of surprise at finding itself a school. Through the tall windows could be seen desks, blackboards, innumerable blazers and panamas festooned on pegs and lines of closely packed wash-basins. Children of varying ages were playing all over the grounds, a confused mass of bright blue, white and grey; here and there a red, gold or black head conspicuous among the predominant light brown. Grainger stopped watching them a moment; they seemed a happy bunch, he thought, and what enviable energy they displayed as they pursued their games with the wholeheartedness of childhood.

As he stood waiting for the headmistress he wondered in what way Sweet's murder would prove to be connected with this peaceful place… how curious though, he thought, is the effect of a school, any type of school on the adult, so familiar and yet so very long ago that the past seems to stretch behind for an enormous distance, as if one had lived not one life, but many.

The door of the common-room opened and he found himself being thoughtfully regarded by a black-haired, leathery-skinned woman with an air of quiet authority.

"Miss Forster?" Grainger inquired.

"Yes. Can I help you?" Her voice was deep and pleasant. "Was it you who wrote to me recently… about the Jonas family?"

"You are quite right, Miss Forster; I am Superintendent Grainger." He took a card from his inside pocket, "I don't know whether you'd like to see this?" Miss Forster waved it away, "No, no. Perhaps you would like to come to my room, and I will tell you all I can. It's only fair to say that I'm not sure whether I shall be free to help you very much, but, of course, that will be easier to judge when you have given me a clearer idea of what you want."

Grainger followed her across the galleried landing to a small light room overlooking the school grounds ringed by agricultural country; it was an austere room, but full of books. With the involuntary gesture of all who love books Grainger leant forward to peer at their titles. He was hampered by politeness and the brilliance of the afternoon sunlight that poured through the window, but they appeared to form a library of social history.

Miss Forster offered him the one armchair and herself sat down at her desk. She took a pair of horn-rimmed spectacles out of the pocket of her plain, dark blue dress and putting them on, bent down to pull open one of the drawers. Selecting a file she opened it out on her desk and frowned down at the contents through her glasses, her mouth setting rather grimly under the puckered skin of her upper lip with its dusting of fine black hairs. Grainger looked across at her thoughtfully, and found himself liking her. She might be a little formidable but she was plainly incorruptibly honest and reliable, the weathering of her face suggested a depth of compassion that hadn't always been easy to bear. Virtually devoid of feminine graces, there was something refreshing in her complete lack of any sort of vanity. Grainger decided that he would need to put his cards on the table; she was accustomed to make her own judgments and perfectly capable of discretion. If he hedged, she would tell him nothing.

Miss Forster raised her chin and took off her glasses; her practised eyes sought the pupils behind his own spectacles before she asked in her pleasant definite manner:

"What did you want to ask, Superintendent?"

He smiled and said, "I think, Miss Forster, I had better tell you my part of the story as it affects the Jonas family; but I can only do that on the understanding that anything I say is for your ear alone."

Miss Forster nodded: "I quite understand, Superintendent. I can assure you that nothing you tell me will ever go any further."

"Thank you. Well, I must tell you then that I have come here because I am investigating a murder. The murdered man was a blackmailer. He kept a skeleton index of his victims which did not in this case include the subject matter on which he was levying blackmail. But this index gave dates and place names referring to such subject matter which have so far proved to be accurate. I am here this morning because under the name Jonas was the address of your school and the date April, 1944."

"I should be interested to know where the blackmailer got his information from… am I permitted to know his name?"

"Ivan Sweet."

"Ivan Sweet." Miss Forster frowned. "No. I have never met anyone of that name." She brooded in silence for a few moments. "Of course it's possible…"

"Yes?" prompted Grainger after a little while.

Miss Forster smiled showing strong white teeth, "Forgive me, Superintendent, I'm always lecturing my pupils about half-finished sentences, I should know better! You have been frank with me and I think the situation demands that I be equally frank with you. But, as far as your work allows, I would like to ask you to respect my confidence as I agreed to respect yours."

"Of course," responded Grainger at once. "I may say," he went on, "that the major part of the information we gather for a murder case never needs to become public, although of course it is essential in building up the pattern that finally gives us our case."

"You are very interested in your work," remarked Miss Forster with approval. "Well, I will tell you what I know of the story as best I can. You will realise I think that in the nature of it, a good deal of what I say will represent my personal opinion, though I may say that my staff felt as I did. However, I want you to allow for this bias, for I felt, and in fact still do feel, very strongly about what happened. Also as you will see there is very little 'hard' proof, it is a tangled, and I'm afraid a tragic story in which the personality of the child Theresa Jonas is the main factor. I will, therefore, tell you the story as it appears to me and leave you to sort out the tangible facts."

"Thank you, Miss Forster, I appreciate your point and shall bear it in mind."

"Well, then, I engaged both Mr. and Mrs. Jonas as members of staff in 1940. I am being frank with you and will therefore add that I would not have done so had it not been for the staffing difficulties during those war years. Theresa was then a small child of three and we took her into the nursery school. I later thought it significant that even at that early age my kindergarten mistress was distressed at her tendency to be spiteful. However, she was very young and we were hardly disposed to take a very serious view of it. And in fact for a time she seemed to improve. I have often felt that this was largely due to the good influence of this particular teacher, who is with us still. She has a great natural talent for rather awkward small children, and little Theresa began to grow fond of her. Unfortunately, in spite of the obvious improvement in the child, her mother bitterly resented this affection and accused Miss Alistair of alienating her daughter's affections; she also, I'm afraid, accused her of a great many other unpleasant things without any foundation whatsoever. I think perhaps life was a little difficult for Mrs. Jonas at this time; we had a pretty young student teacher here then, and I regret to say that Mr. Jonas paid her much more attention than was proper in a married man. I can say now that I tried very hard to replace both the Jonas's at this time, but staffing difficulties became more and more severe and in the end I kept them on. I was to regret this decision deeply. However, for the time being things went on reasonably quietly; those were hard and worrying years as we all remember, and there was plenty to think about outside the school day. From time to time it was my duty to break the news to some poor child of a father or brother killed or captured..." She was silent for a moment and her face so faithfully mirrored that terrible time that Grainger, too, felt himself transported back. She raised her head and looked at him with her honest, melancholy eyes.

"One day I had to call two little sisters up here to my room. Their father had been killed in Burma. They took it well, as all the children did, but I knew the ache, the emptiness and the fear they must feel, for all their courage, and I had a word with their form masters as I usually did. One of these masters was a very kindly young Irishman, a Mr. Connerly. He was also Theresa's form master. All his class were very fond of him, he had a sympathetic personality and with so many fathers away from home the tendency to fasten affections on a master was rather stronger than in normal times. It is perfectly natural, but always a problem to handle where small girls are concerned. They rather easily become competitive and jealous in their affections. Mr. Connerly was very anxious to give any comfort he could to little Joanna who had lost her father and Theresa Jonas, who was also in his class, reacted with increasing jealousy. I have blamed myself bitterly for not realising the lengths to which this was to push her, but she was only seven and although her behaviour was disturbed and unpleasant, I thought it would pass if we didn't take too much notice. Unfortunately I was wrong. Joanna was a pretty and a popular child and this, too, doubtless inflamed Theresa who was always rather a sallow and gawky girl." Miss Forster rubbed her finger-tips over her forehead as if to push away the thoughts that troubled her.

"It all came to a head one break in April, 1944. In the playground we have two big trees in which some of the bigger boys have built a wooden hut. It is very popular with all the children and the trees are not dangerous to climb, so this has never been forbidden. Also we always have one of the staff on duty near by. On this occasion Mrs. Jonas was on duty." Grainger looked up and Miss Forster nodded.

"Yes," she said, "that was to make everything even more difficult, I was in here; it was almost the end of term and I was working on reports. I could hear the children playing and shouting as they always do in break and I thought how quiet it was going to be next week when they had all gone home for Easter. And then there was a scream"—she shook her head as if she could hear it still—"and afterwards absolute silence. I rushed out to the playground and saw a crowd of children standing under the two big trees looking down at something on the ground. When I reached them I saw what they were staring at. Joanna was lying there and she was quite still. I thought she was dead. It would have been better if she had been.

"Our doctor lives very near. I sent someone to fetch him while I knelt down to see if there was anything I could do. Up in the tree above me, someone started to sob. I looked up and saw Susan, Joanna's little sister and next to her Theresa Jonas. I still would like to think that I imagined the expression on Theresa's face. I must have been overwrought, no child of seven should look like that. Our head boy was standing near me. I asked him to go up into the trees and very carefully help little Susan down, she was only five. Then Theresa spoke. She said, 'I didn't do it.' And her mother said at once, 'No, of course you didn't, it was Susan who pushed her.' I gave her such a look as I have never turned on anyone, and then the doctor came. I asked my kindergarten mistress to take Susan to my room and sent everybody back to their classrooms. When Dr. Harper examined Joanna, I saw her eyelids flutter, and

I thanked God that she was alive. I didn't know then that she would be paralysed from her neck down for the rest of her life."

Grainger was silent. At length he said:

"Thank you, Miss Forster. It's a horrible story. Is she still alive?"

"Yes. And I have Susan here still. As you remember the father was killed on active service; as if everything else weren't enough they are now very poor. The mother can't go out to work when she has a cripple at home to look after. I do what little I can by having Susan here and looking after Joanna sometimes in the school holidays. I shall always feel that I should have foreseen and prevented what happened."

"Nobody could have done so," said Grainger with finality. He paused a moment before asking, "There was no attempt to claim compensation from the Jonas's?"

Miss Forster shook her head, "As you may imagine, there were endless discussions about that. I took legal advice, as a matter of fact my brother is a barrister, and I think we would have succeeded. But Mrs. Jonas continued to accuse Susan. My brother said that accusation would have been broken down in court, but the little girl's mother felt that for Susan to have to be accused and cross-examined publicly, even though they won their case, would do her so much harm at five years old, that she preferred to drop it and manage as best she could. We got up a subscription, of course, and many people have been very kind… but… nothing can undo what has been done to that family."

"No." There was a pause while Miss Forster relived the past and Grainger measured up this horrid tale against his case. At length he said, "Was Joanna questioned about what happened?"

"Yes. She said that Theresa pushed her. We asked if she had seen Theresa pushing her, and she said no, she was pushed violently from behind, but she knew it was Theresa because Theresa was always trying to hurt her and obviously it wouldn't have been Susan. The two sisters were always very fond of each other and became even more attached after their father was killed. Later she said that Theresa had threatened to kill her if she didn't stop making up to Mr. Connerly."

Grainger nodded slowly. "Right in the beginning, Miss Forster, before you told me all this, when you were wondering how the blackmailer got to know the story, you began to say, 'Of course it's possible…' And then you stopped. Could you tell me what you had in mind?"

Miss Forster frowned, "Oh yes, I know," she said, "I was going to say, of course it's possible the blackmailer might have found out from the child herself. Naturally we got rid of the three of them the next day. I only wish I had acted earlier," she said again, and Grainger realised it was an obsession with her and was sorry; the fault hadn't been hers.

"We used to find that when Theresa was being spiteful," the headmistress went on, "she was inclined to boast about the damage she'd done. She was quite fantastically vain and would boast about things most people would be ashamed to advertise."

"Thank you. That's very interesting. Did you ever hear any more of the Jonas family after they left the school?"

"No. Not a word until your letter came yesterday. Not unnaturally they didn't apply to us for a reference. Do you know if they're both teaching still?"

"Only Mr. Jonas."

She nodded. "He was a fool, and a philanderer, but nothing worse." She grinned suddenly, "I *am* being frank, Superintendent, are you using a truth drug?"

"If there is such a thing, it certainly wouldn't be necessary to use it on you."

Miss Forster smiled absently, "Superintendent?" she said suddenly. "You will have seen Theresa quite recently, won't you?"

"Yes, very recently."

Miss Forster hesitated. "Having met her yourself, does it seem feasible to you that this story I have told you could have happened? Or have we all of us down here got it out of perspective?"

Grainger met her eyes gravely. "To be quite honest, Miss Forster, I don't think you have it in the least out of perspective. As you spoke the girl's face was often before me, I fear your story was only too convincing... You may be interested to know that she pushed a neighbour's pretty child out of a tree a year or two ago. She was thrashed for it by the child's elder brother whose opinion of her matches yours to a remarkable degree."

Miss Forster shook her head worriedly. "I can't help feeling I have a responsibility there. I know what she's capable of, at least I honestly think I do, and I've got her away from my school, but suppose she does it again? What can I possibly do, Superintendent?"

"It's an extremely delicate position," said Grainger slowly. "But it's certainly not your responsibility, Miss Forster. Even if it had ever been, which it hasn't, it would cease now that you have told me the story." He took out his pipe and lit it in response to Miss Forster's acquiescent smile. Blowing a cloud of smoke through his nostrils he said, "I don't feel satisfied that Joanna is receiving no compensation; you understand, Miss Forster, that I am speaking very much off the record, but it would give me personal satisfaction to look into that even if it isn't strictly my province. After all, these things don't have to get into court if the case is strong enough. Also as Susan grows up she may herself feel she wants to take some action about it…"

"It's interesting that you should say that," Miss Forster broke in, "because she said something of the sort to me only a short while ago."

"Did she? Is your brother still interested in the case, do you think? I would like to get his opinion on it."

"Oh yes, I'm sure he is. James always thought we should have gone ahead with it, but I myself did very much see the mother's point of view."

"I would be glad to have his name and telephone number and the address of Joanna's mother."

Miss Forster hesitated. "I don't like to do anything that might serve to remind them of that time."

Grainger said in a voice he didn't often use:

"I'm afraid every minute of every day must remind them of that time; and money does help, especially to make life bearable for a cripple."

The headmistress looked at him without speaking and nodded. She wrote the two addresses down on a card and gave it to the policeman.

They walked together down the stairs and through the hall with its characteristic school smell of chalk and ink and faint wafts from 'stinks', rubber boots and hot blazers, cricket-bat oil and disinfectant polish; and out into the grounds which smelt of hot grass and sun-warmed weatherboarding from the pavilion across the field.

"Those are the trees." Miss Forster pointed to two close-growing oaks joined up in the boughs by a stout wooden platform on which a small house was built. His eyes travelled up into the branches imagining the bony face of the girl Theresa peering down with hideous triumph at the rival she had hated. At seven years old! Is the killer-type born and not made, he wondered?

# SEVENTEEN

"I SNA' YON THE KIDDY?" ASKED MCGREGOR OF HIS CHIEF, slowing the car as they passed the park. He pointed to a thin figure standing by the gates. Grainger blinked at it through his glasses.

"Yes, Mac, you're quite right, it is. Pull up, will you?" He frowned as he regarded the girl who was peering furtively through the railings and shrubs although the park gates stood open at her side. She was a distressing spectacle, her forehead pressed against the bars, displaying the back of a narrow head divided by a bony-white parting and ending in a thin neck and a protuberant vertebra. Her lean bottom stuck out above spindly legs as she peered in with feverish intensity. While they still watched, she drew away from her peephole and minced in through the park gates.

"Take a stroll in the park, will you, Mac?" asked Grainger. "I'd be interested to know what she gets up to on her own; and if you get a good opportunity, try her out on what happened at that school."

"It'll be a pleasure," replied the Scot grimly. The memory of the patient living head on the wasted wreck of a child's body had refused to leave him since his visit to the injured Joanna. He levered his big form out of the car, and, assuming a dilatory calm which made the watching Grainger smile, sauntered in through the park gates. The Superintendent moved into the driver's seat and drove on to Magnolia Cottage.

The speed with which the front door was opened this time reminded him that he had been parked outside for some few moments and had doubtless been under close observation.

"Oh, Superintendent, I'm so glad you called, I have news of the very first importance for you; in fact it seems more than probable that I have solved your case for you." Still talking Mrs. Jonas led him into the room he remembered from his previous visit. Her husband was hovering uncomfortably in the gloom, his expression apprehensive.

"I learned yesterday afternoon something that made me wish to come down to you at Scotland Yard at once, but unfortunately my husband prefers to leave trouble alone; I tell him he has not a sufficiently developed sense of civic responsibility." She directed a scornful glance at him, and, looking increasingly uncomfortable, he muttered, "Well, dear, if you want to talk to the superintendent I think I'll go out and buy a packet of cigarettes."

"I'm afraid I must ask you to remain, sir. I have some questions to put to you and your wife." Grainger's voice was quiet but final, and Edouard Jonas's narrow form collapsed into a chair. He murmured vaguely, "Oh, I see, quite so, I didn't realise." He glanced nervously at his formidable wife.

"Your questions can wait, Superintendent. This news I have for you is of vital importance. You will see that when I tell you what it is."

"I should be very glad if you would do so," returned Grainger woodenly. Those who knew him could have warned Mrs. Jonas that this exceptionally quiet Grainger was a dangerous man. Not that Mrs. Jonas was a woman to accept warnings from anyone.

"I have discovered the motive for this murder, Inspector," she announced dramatically, demoting the police officer in her excitement.

"Oh, yes?"

Poor fool, he knows he should have unearthed this himself, the woman's contemptuous face proclaimed. She continued importantly, "That woman at Magnolia House is not Mr. Southey's wife, whatever she may think of her precious husband, and all those abominably behaved brats of hers are illegitimates!" Her hatred and triumph painted the words in livid scarlet on the dingy air of the little room.

"I imagine you know"—her tone implied that she was sure he did not—"that Mrs. Southey is a Catholic. Poor Ivan Sweet discovered that that pompous fraud is a bigamist, and he had no sooner discovered it than he was murdered, in that house!" She stood there in dumpy arrogance, an ill-disguised sneer on her unlovely mouth, triumphing over the stupid men who were staring at her, her husband with open fear, Grainger with a total lack of expression. There was a silence. "Well, what do you think of that?" she demanded.

"I think, madam," replied Grainger coolly, "that if you are incapable of exercising more control over your tongue, you will find yourself arraigned for slander. If not for something more serious," he added thoughtfully regarding her with a hard stare.

"That's just what I told you, dear..." began Mr. Jonas before he crumpled beneath his wife's furious explosion. When it was over, Grainger took out a notebook and pencil and asked, "On what grounds do you make these very grave allegations, Mrs. Jonas?"

"You'd do better to go and arrest them before they murder someone else than waste time cross-examining me," retorted Mrs. Jonas furiously.

"Arrest who?"

The woman directed a withering glance at him.

"The Southeys, of course. Who else could it be?"

Grainger raised his eyebrows, "You suggest I arrest the whole family?"

"This is scarcely an occasion for levity, Inspector. A man has been murdered."

"I assure you, madam, I had not lost sight of the fact. Your suggestion is that I arrest some unspecified number of the Southey family for the murder of Ivan Sweet?"

"For heaven's sake!" Edouard Jonas burst out in alarm; he turned to Grainger, "Of course my wife means nothing of the sort. As you can see she is a little overwrought…"

"I am nothing of the sort!" she screamed. "Are those people to get away with anything, even murder?"

"Am I to understand that you witnessed one of these people killing Mr. Sweet?" Grainger inquired mildly.

"Of course I didn't. Do you think they'd be fools enough to do it in front of witnesses? But it's obvious to any fool that one of them did it. Look at their motive!"

"Even supposing that some member of that family had a motive for killing Ivan Sweet, they would not be alone in that. You yourselves had a motive for silencing him; that is why I am here now. We will raise that matter when we have dealt with this. Now will you kindly answer my earlier question, what are your grounds for the allegations you have made?"

"You must be wandering, Inspector. What possible reason

could we have for killing Ivan?" But there was panic now under her fury, and her husband was in a pitiable state, crouched in his chair biting his nails, his face paper-white.

"You have not answered my question," Grainger reminded them equably.

"Oh, well, if you must know, but as a matter of fact I was told in confidence. That woman is so mealy-mouthed… she didn't want it to go any further, she said, because they're her friends. Nice friends I must say. Anyway you'll have to see what you can get out of her."

"Out of whom?" Grainger inquired patiently.

"Mrs. Moore, of course. I told you. Ivan told her that he knew Southey had another wife living quite a short time before the murder."

"I see." Grainger's tone was icy. "So your allegations of bigamy and murder were based on hearsay?"

"That's what I told you, but you would go on," mumbled Edouard from his chair. Grainger's eyes flicked over him and back to the woman.

"Well, Mrs. Jonas, if you wish to avoid a slander case, I would recommend that you keep a very much stricter watch on your tongue than would seem to be your habit." He looked down at them both inimically. "And now," he went on, "for the questions I came here to ask." He paused deliberately to assess their apprehension and was aware of the woman's venomous alarmed china-blue stare and the narrow little man's shifting nervous glances at his closed lips.

"Why," he asked, "did you not inform me that you were being blackmailed by Ivan Sweet?"

There was a moment's silence before Barbara Jonas answered haughtily, "I don't understand you, Inspector." Grainger glanced at her with *ennui*, blinking his sandy lashes. "I will put it another way," he said. "Why did you pay out several quite considerable sums to Ivan Sweet after he threatened to advertise an accident in which you and your daughter were involved at Allanshurst School?"

The two Jonas's exchanged a rapid glance, but Barbara pulled herself together at once, "I fail to understand you, Inspector. There was an inquiry into that accident at the time and it was found that the child had been injured by her own sister."

"Oh, no, Mrs. Jonas, there was no such finding. The only person who has ever made such an accusation is yourself, and moreover I suggest to you that you did not at any time yourself believe that Susan was responsible."

"This is outrageous!" Mrs. Jonas's sallow skin was flaming in angry patches from her greasy hairline to her discoloured neck.

"Many things are outrageous," remarked Grainger rather wearily. "Sweet was a methodical blackmailer and kept account of his profits. You made him three payments of twenty pounds, one very shortly before he was murdered…"

"If you're suggesting that I killed him to avoid paying him I should scarcely leave the money on him, would I?" interrupted Barbara Jonas triumphantly.

Grainger's eyes rested on her without expression. "It might not have been convenient to remove it," he said casually. "How did you know that your twenty pounds was still in the flat when he died?"

Barbara shrugged her shoulders. "It hardly seems likely that he would have had time to spend it."

"At what time did you give it to him?"

"Oh… about nine I suppose."

"On which day?"

"On Friday night of course. He was never up by that time in the morning."

"Have you found your hypodermic syringe yet, Mrs. Jonas?"

"Of course I haven't. I've never had such a thing. I told your sergeant so when he came here blethering about it."

"Well, that is all I need to ask you for the moment." Grainger put away his notebook and turned towards the door.

"Oh... Superintendent," Edouard's nervous tenor sounded behind him; Grainger turned back, "Yes, Mr. Jonas?"

"Er—the—er—sixty pounds my wife paid over to Sweet... will this be returned?"

Grainger's eyes regarded him thoughtfully. "Oh yes, Mr. Jonas, it'll be returned in due course."

Christine Southey was standing in the cloister doorway and ran down to Grainger as he approached his car, "Could you please come in a moment?" she asked. "Mummy's found something."

The child led him up to her father's studio. Caroline said, "You were perfectly right, Superintendent, we've just found a hypodermic syringe, though how it came to be here is a complete mystery to us all. I've just been asking the others about it. It's in there, look"—she pointed—"in that shiny little box. I'm afraid I've touched it because I didn't know what it was. As a matter of fact the baby found it, he picked it up and I took it from him to see what he had got."

Grainger crouched down to look at the little box among the tubes of paint and other litter on the shelf.

"You've no idea how long it's been here?" he asked. Caroline shook her head rather helplessly.

"No, I'm afraid I haven't," she answered. "Oddly enough I made a start on turning this room out, on the day Yo... er—a friend was taken ill and I was called away before I got to these shelves."

Grainger had noted the bitten-off name.

"Perhaps that would have been Miss Yolande Meade who is now in hospital," he suggested. "That would have been on Wednesday last."

The police officer was aware of the family's defensive shrinking away from him at this reminder of intimate police surveillance, but Caroline merely said in a rather withdrawn tone, "Yes, you are quite right, Superintendent, it was on Wednesday."

"And you definitely did not notice this little box here then?"

"No... But that doesn't mean it wasn't there; I didn't reach these shelves." She frowned perplexedly: "It seems so extraordinary that you should have asked about it only yesterday when I had no idea there was such a thing in the house, and it should have turned up today."

Grainger smiled rather grimly, "Yes," he agreed, "it does seem extraordinary, doesn't it?" He regarded the little box thoughtfully. "Would you like to see how we test for finger-prints?" he asked Christine.

He blew on the fine white dust and five pairs of eyes watched a thumb-print and four tiny finger-prints emerge from the whitened surface. "That's where your Mummy and your little brother picked it up just now," Grainger explained. "If we turn it over we shall see the marks of baby's thumb and some of Mummy's fingers; there, you see? We'll just ask Mummy to put her fingermarks on this glass"—he took a small mirror from his pocket—"and then you can see how they have the same little lines on them." Caroline handed the glass back to him and the children compared the whitened prints with interest.

"What about Desmond's?" asked Christine.

"Oh, I don't think we need bother Desmond for his," answered Grainger smiling.

"There's a glass thing inside, like the doctor uses when you have to have an injection, wouldn't there be any on that?" Christine pursued.

"Maybe. But I shall look at those at Scotland Yard," replied Grainger firmly. He turned to the others.

"Do you think you could give me a complete list of all the people who have been, or could have been, in this room since yesterday morning?"

"All of us have been here to start with," William Southey's deep voice sounded for the first time, "and Mrs. Lion, I suppose"—he looked interrogatively at his wife.

"Oh, yes, she would have been. But it isn't easy to remember who else, everything is so confused. Let me think now"—she rubbed her hands over her forehead as if she were trying to see the events of the last twenty-four hours played out against the darkness of her eyes.

"I know," said Christine, "yesterday Mr. Meade was here telling us about Aunty Yolande, and Mrs. Moore came down to borrow some China tea and it was yesterday evening Dickey said he'd found Theresa in the hall and turned her out."

"And wasn't it yesterday morning that nice big lady with black hair and a deep voice came to see you, Mummy?" the child added suddenly.

Caroline gazed at her in distress, "So she did. Oh, dear, I oughtn't to have forgotten that, I meant to tell you, Will, that poor girl Patrick Sweet's wife—she's got a little girl of three and a tiny baby and they're practically starving. Apparently they were on their beam ends when they were here that night at the party, and since then Patrick has hardly been home at all. Rachel Saunders came round yesterday about it."

"There may be some public assistance for a case like that; I'll have it looked into," Grainger said.

Out in the street again Grainger saw that McGregor had not returned to the car, and he wandered up the hill and turned into the road by the park. The bright weather was breaking and the clustering leaves of the deciduous trees and the luxuriant heads of the summer flowers were taking a tossing from the rough wind. Beyond the ruffled waters of the lake a resplendent old cedar took the blustering breeze with a statelier grace.

Paul Grainger walked slowly down one of the main pathways, keeping a wary eye open for McGregor. The green rustling darkness that precedes an English summer storm was deepening over the pretty little park. For a moment the sun gleamed out again, a brilliant yellow-green light slanting out under the edge of a thunder-cloud and lending all objects that vividness of perspective that the slanting lights of dawn and sunset bring. Suddenly Grainger stopped and then moved quietly back under the cover of a wildly bowing lilac, dark and dull until next spring crowned it with scented plumes again. He had caught sight of McGregor sitting on a seat with Theresa. She was consuming ice-cream and talking with dreadful animation.

He watched them for a few moments and then walked quietly back to the road. A tall figure was entering the park gates as he came up to them; it seemed familiar and he and Henry Meade recognised each other at the same moment. The old man seemed somewhat taken aback. He raised his hat, gave Grainger a 'good evening' and walked slowly on into the park. About to cross the road outside, the detective suddenly heard the old man's footsteps returning. He turned round and saw Meade walking purposefully towards him.

"I—I'd like to speak with you a moment if I may, Superintendent."

"Of course, Mr. Meade. My car isn't far away, would you care to come and sit in it?"

"No, thank you. What I have to tell you will take no more than a moment." He paused, and Grainger was aware of the thin old chest moving fast in and out with his agitated breathing. With an effort, Meade started to speak again.

"I feel I ought to regard this chance meeting as providential, Superintendent. I... I was about to do something both wrong and foolish." He took a small package from his pocket and thrust it at Grainger as if he feared for the persistence of his own resolution. The package was heavy. Grainger weighed it in his hand and turned it over.

"I weighted it with sand so that it would sink," said the old man speaking rapidly but more easily.

"You will find it is a hypodermic syringe; my dear wife was a diabetic and I have always retained this syringe which she was accustomed to use, poor darling. One of your men told me yesterday that you were inquiring among all of us who were—involved with Mr. Sweet, about the possession of a hypodermic. In the circumstances I am ashamed to admit that I almost yielded to the temptation to dispose of it."

Grainger thanked him gravely. "It was not only a right, but also a wise decision to hand this over to me, Mr. Meade. We should certainly have found it." He paused, "I hope your daughter is making good progress?"

Meade's faded blue eyes regarded him searchingly.

"Thank you, Superintendent. I am happy to say that she is."

Grainger nodded, "I'm glad to hear it." He put the package in his pocket and raised his hat. "Good-bye," he said. He watched the tall lonely figure for a few moments as he walked up the street towards his cottage. The past week had added years to the old man's age. Grainger sighed and crossed the road.

McGregor was sitting in the driving seat, his face full of news. "Back to the Yard, is it, sir?" the Scot inquired, as soon as Grainger was settled in his seat.

"Please, Mac." He took out his pipe and pouch. "Out with it, Mac, what have you got?" He smiled at the sergeant.

"Ugh!" responded Mac with a shudder. "It's some sort of a hell-bairn that. For what it's worth to us she admits pushin' that puir lassie out o' the tree. Very proud o' hersel' she was, no one stands in her way but they've to pay for it, that's her doctrine. Mind ye I told some pretty tales mysel' to get her goin', I thocht I was pitchin' it o'er strong, but ye should ha' seen her lappin' it up, along wi' a mort o' that ice-cream I had to buy her—that's goin' on expenses… three o' them she demolished!"

Grainger laughed.

"She'd a bag o' sweets, too," Mac continued. "She pinched them from a wee bairn oot wi' her sister no mich older than hersel'. Sakes but I wanted to gi'e her a spankin'—bit it wouldna' ha' been a guid introduction," he added sadly.

Grainger laughed again, "Indeed it wouldn't," he agreed. "You know if she feels like that about it, her parents must have had a job to make her hold her tongue all these years. My guess is she's talked about it from time to time and no one's believed her.

Except Ivan Sweet, of course; that's probably how he got hold of the story. Did she say anything about him?"

"Noo. I tried her but she wouldna' say a thing."

"Hmm. Wonder if she's seen anything that frightened her? Doesn't sound in character to be so uncommunicative." He smoked in silence for a few moments.

"What did ye get from the parents?" inquired McGregor.

"Oh, it was interesting if not elevating. Mrs. Jonas has got wind of poor Southey's bigamy. That Moore woman told her." He laughed, "I'm a fine policeman, aren't I, putting it that way! They were both pretty alarmed when I came back at them with the stuff we got yesterday, but though it's possible, and I'd put nothing past her, especially if she planned to let one of the Southeys wear the rope for her, neither the opportunity nor the motive are as strong as theirs, that's the hell of it. A hypodermic's turned up in that studio. No prints on the box except Mrs. Southey's and the baby's... they found it. We'll have a look at the syringe itself when we get back, but I'll be surprised if we find anything. Then there's old Meade; he's just handed me another. Admitted he was about to dispose of it! That pretty daughter of his is in hospital with a miscarriage. There's no lack of motive there, and he'd have counted it worth stopping a marriage to Ivan Sweet even if he had to hang for it." Grainger chewed at his pipe stem frowning. "There's a bit missing somewhere you know, Mac, I think, and I'm pretty sure it's connected with that old legacy from Mildred Price. Incidentally, the present heir is behaving even more oddly than usual. He's hardly been home since the inquest and his wife and children are on the verge of starvation. No hypodermic from there so far. What the poor woman will do with it if she finds one I don't know, but we'll pick it up if she tries to get rid of it."

"Och, weel," remarked Mac comfortably, "we've not been on it a full week yet. The Commissioner will give us a bit o' latitude the while afore he starts agitatin' about an arrest." He swung the car into the Yard park and the burly figure and the slim one made their way into the big grey building, while outside the London traffic pounded by in the gathering gloom of the approaching storm, and the hurrying summer-clad crowds heard the first distant rumble of thunder and glanced up at the threatening sky.

# EIGHTEEN

EVEN AMONG THE RUMBLE AND CLANG OF TROLLEYS AND lifts through the big hospital, the thunder sounded, a premonitory roar from the larger elements outside. The very small boy who held his cut hand stiffly for Jonathon to stitch turned his head towards the sound, his eyes wide with alarm.

"Don't you like the thunder bow-wow?" Jon asked persuasively, trying not to wince himself as he threaded the curved needle through the little fellow's skin to draw the gaping edges of the gash together. The child shook his head without speaking.

"But he's a fine fellow; he never hurts, you know, only barks very, very loudly and strikes big matches to light up the sky when he feels mischievous." The child's creamy forehead stirred in a baby's frown.

"Wot's mis... mis...?"

"Mischievous?" Jonathon felt himself sweating with the effort of this new form of social intercourse. Elaine would know what to say, he thought, Elaine... he sighed unconsciously.

"There," he said when he'd tied the last stitch, "now you be careful of that hand till those little stitches have grown together again."

The child regarded his hand with interest.

"Will gwow?" he inquired.

"All that nice skin'll grow together again, just like new if you take care of it and keep it nice and clean." The thunder pealed again, nearer this time; the small boy frowned.

"Got ver' loud voice," he remarked censoriously.

"He's such a long way off up on the clouds we wouldn't be able to hear him if he didn't shout."

"Mmm."

"Bye-bye."

Jonathon took out his handkerchief and wiped the sweat from his neck and forehead. It crossed his mind that perhaps he wasn't suited to be a father. He frowned, Elaine would certainly want children.

He turned to his next patient, an old bent woman who asked in a quavering voice to have her ears syringed. At least there won't be any conversation required this time, he thought gratefully as he prepared the syringe and in this he was right, for his patient's one requirement was to be allowed to talk. She wavered on, fragile but inexorable, like a cracked and rusty musical box whose motor has mysteriously found the secret of perpetual motion. As Jonathon gradually loosened plugs of black wax from her pale papery ear, her tinkle of domestic anecdotes built up tenuous pictures in his mind, as intangible as reflections in bubbles, for the old lady wandered in and out of decades and generations with the facility of the very old. How shrunken and limp her flesh is, he thought, remembering the plump, tautly filled skin of the tiny boy's hand he had been stitching just before. Even more than death, who must be the familiar of every hospital, the contrast of youth and age brought him face to face with mortality, pricking through an unarmoured crack in the specialised imagination medical students grow like a second skin over their native shrinking. And Elaine and I are wasting whole days of living being miserable over silly trifles, he thought. I'll ring her up as soon as I get clear here.

The swing doors opened to admit two stretcher bearers carrying a cherry-pink man, breathing stertorously.

Oh, Lord, a gas poisoning, Jonathon thought, and something stirred at the back of his mind as he tackled his next case, a girl of sixteen or seventeen with roving eyes and a septic hand. It was bad and he went off to get permission to inject penicillin from the senior casualty officer who was attending to the gas poisoning. He stood, tall and young and unscathed, looking down at the pathetic stressed body of the old man, still reeking of gas and wondered how he had come to lie pink and gasping on a stretcher, his life in other hands. Suddenly the latent memory took shape, it was something Elaine had told him about Mrs. Moore, the woman who lived in the attics. She had been gassed while she slept only a week or two before the murder, and what's more, he thought, recovering from that, she had inexplicably fallen down the steep flight of stairs from her flat. He obtained his permission, fetched his penicillin and returned to his case to give the injection, automatically producing his 'injection' patter to soothe the girl, who was eyeing the needle with dislike. He became absorbed in finding a suitable bundle of muscle into which to inject the antibiotic. The girl grinned and chattered with relief when it was over, making eyes at him crudely and somehow pathetically. He smiled at her with a patience that he hoped wouldn't strike her as superiority and gently and deftly removed the dressings on the hot swollen hand with its incongruous painted claws. Disraeli was right enough about the two nations, he thought, but I don't know what the dickens one does about it. His mind returned to the murder at Magnolia House, and he thought uneasily of Elaine's story of her father's possible involvement with Ivan Sweet. Southey fitted all his conceptions of what a moral man should be, but he was also a man of single-minded determination… supposing he had in fact an urgent reason for wanting Sweet out of the way? It was criminal of me to quarrel with Elaine at a time like this, the poor kid must be under a tremendous strain. Unwanted, other thoughts pushed themselves towards definition in his mind… what was it that made them flare so easily into heated disagreement… and then… of course it shouldn't really make any difference but supposing her father proved in fact to be a murderer… he pushed the treacherous thought from his mind. If only I could ring her now he thought; he glanced at his watch, nearly four o'clock. Not long now.

"Hallo…" said Elaine, picking up the phone. Her voice changed, "Oh, Jon, it's you…" The phone buzzed emphatically. "Oh, darling, of course I do. It wasn't you, anyway, it was me… I've nearly rung a score of times to say so…"

"Well, it was both of us then… No, we won't, will we, Jon? I can't think why we did…"

"Darling… you had an idea about what?"

"Mrs. Moore?"

"When she was gassed you mean?"

"Oh, it must have been about a couple of weeks before."

"Yes, I suppose it's possible… but I can't imagine any connection, can you?"

"Hmm… well, it's all so impossibly mysterious I suppose it's worth trying…"

"Yes, she apparently fell down the whole flight…"

"Oh, it was only a day or two after the first accident. I remember wondering whether she was still feeling unsteady on her feet…"

"Well, that would be lovely anyway, darling... by six? Oh, what a shame... but we'd have an hour or so... I'll drive down to you and then we can have longer. Say in fifteen minutes, then. God bless, darling."

"I'm so hot!" said the child again, so pitifully that Phoebe Sweet's heart contracted as she bent over the cot and smoothed back the tangle of damp hair. She *was* hot, burning hot. In his basket in the corner the baby was quietly crying for his feed. Phoebe looked worriedly at her watch, a present from Pat in days so long ago that they seemed to have no reality now. I ought to have fed him half an hour ago, she thought. Worries fretted at the confusion and anxiety that filled her mind. If only Pat were here he could at least fetch a doctor, she thought, but God knows where he's got to, or when he'll be back. I wish I could take her temperature... suddenly she remembered a first-aid kit, a relic of Pat's R.A.M.C. days. There might be a thermometer in that...

"Daddy said"—the thin high voice was slurred with fever— "Daddy said soon we'd have lots of pennies because we could have Uncle Ivan's now he's dead... How did he die, Mummy?"

Phoebe stopped rummaging in the trunk and kept quite still. "Oh, he—he—his heart stopped, darling. Don't you worry your head about it... when did Daddy say that, Janice?"

"Don't know... p'raps the other day... so hot, time goes messy."

Mechanically Phoebe's hands began to search again. Her fingers found hard edges. She drew out a box and wrenched back the lid. Inside was a chaotic jumble. As she searched for the thermometer she turned up something at the bottom of the box. She sat down suddenly and heard her own voice saying, "Oh God. No!"

The baby's hungry wail finally roused her and with trembling hands she put the thermometer under the little girl's tongue. The half minute ticked endlessly on while the questions raged in her head. She slipped the tube out. One hundred and four. Oh God, she said again.

Someone was knocking at the door. Phoebe looked round wildly. Snatching up the hypodermic she thrust it back into the box and threw the first-aid box back in the trunk... weak for lack of food she was reeling with the effort of rapid movement. Oh God, if it were the police!

The knock came again. Phoebe glanced at the sick child, alarmed suddenly by her quietness and saw that she was snatching some sleep away from the heat and pain at last. Fearfully she went to the door.

But it was only Caroline who stood there, rather embarrassed, with a hamper of food.

Twenty minutes later, as she leant back on freshly plumped pillows, a tray on her lap, Phoebe decided she must be dreaming. Janice still slept fitfully, and Caroline had gone to fetch the doctor. Her body was crying out for the fragrant food and the sharpness of her fears was becoming rapidly blunted. "I must have been hysterical to think such a thing of Pat," she decided, and picked up her spoon.

Phoebe's momentary sense of hope would not have been possible if she could have seen her husband at that moment.

Pat scarcely knew any more who he was or what he did; beyond fatigue and almost beyond fear, his feet in their broken shoes trod the endless pavements of London while his problem gyrated in his mind with a sickening speed. He was completely unable to come to any decision. People looked after him curiously as his gaunt shabby figure rustled by and some shivered to see his face. Perhaps his feet knew the answer to the question he couldn't resolve, for they walked him at last into Scotland Yard. And when he found himself there he knew what he had to do.

# NINETEEN

"**I** DARE SAY THEY WERE JUST A COUPLE OF UNRELATED ACCI-dents, but it could have been attempted murder, couldn't it? If by any chance we were right, she'd almost certainly be in danger…"

"But wouldn't there have been another attempt in that case?" Elaine asked.

"Not necessarily." Jonathon finished his tea thoughtfully and put down his cup. "The killer might be afraid to make a move while the police are vigorously investigating the murder of Sweet."

Elaine felt her scalp prickling with apprehension.

"I think you're right, Jon, we ought to tell the superintendent."

"All right, let's go."

As the car neared Scotland Yard, Elaine began to look uncomfortable. "I hope he doesn't think we're a couple of busy-bodies," she remarked uneasily.

"Doesn't matter if he does," responded Jonathon, who was thinking in the same terms himself. "Still, I think we should tell him, so devil take the consequences, hmm?"

"Mm," agreed Elaine rather breathily. They got out of the car and walked up to the big building, feeling very young and inexperienced.

But Grainger quickly put them at their ease. He listened soberly to what Jonathon had to say and questioned Elaine in detail about the two accidents. Finally he thanked them gravely and told the girl that he would be at Magnolia House later that evening.

They drove away with mixed feelings. Something indefinable in the superintendent's manner had suggested that the case was very near its conclusion and they became increasingly silent as they drove northwards to Elaine's home. Jonathon glanced rather anxiously at his watch.

"The devil of it is I promised to be back at the hospital at six," he said, "but I expect I could excuse myself..."

"No, darling, you go," responded Elaine at once. "In fact there's no need for you to take me back. I shall be home in a quarter of an hour."

"No, I'm going to see you safely home first, but I'll get through as fast as I can and come out again if I may."

"Please, Jon, I'd like it very much."

He looked at her, "Don't worry, sweetheart. It'll soon be over now."

"Yes. Yes it will, won't it." The question of how it would be over hung over them both unspoken, an incalculable shape, coloured with menace. They were at the bottom of the hill now, the lights changed, the traffic revved and roared upwards. As the house came into view upon the summit their hearts jolted uneasily, like aircraft in an air pocket. Then they were outside. Jonathon took Elaine's hands and held them hard in his own.

"I'll be back soon, sweetheart."

"Yes, darling." They exchanged a long look.

"I don't like to leave you—I'm damned if I will..."

"Yes, darling, you must, please. It's important." She smiled rather shyly, "I'm going to be a surgeon's wife, aren't I? Let's begin as we mean to go on. You'll be back soon."

He kissed her hard and she watched him race off down the hill and jump on a moving bus. He turned on the platform and waved to her, and she watched his tall figure and red head and the white waving hand receding into the distance until the bus was lost among all the other traffic revving and braking in a noisy tangle up and down the hill. She turned when at last it was useless to look any longer, and as she did so the foreboding that while Jonathon was there she had kept at arm's length, closed in and took possession of her. She looked up at the old house for the comfort it always gave her, and there was no comfort. The windows looked blankly at her and she saw menace in their blankness. The high windy sky raced by above the towering roofs and the vast building seemed to sway towards her so that she stepped back involuntarily. She laughed at herself for succumbing to the visual illusion, but her laughter was hollow and tangled with the breath which she could no longer draw calmly. She sucked the air in through opened lips, trying to still the fluttering of her heart which seemed as if it must burst her chest and wished wildly that she could call Jonathon back. But it was too late. She pulled off her hat and ran an icy hand through her hair and forced herself to walk through the cloister door into the waiting house. Inside it was quite silent. She walked slowly upstairs, resolved to go to her room and try to calm herself before she faced anyone. High up on the second floor, she lingered by the landing window looking down the hill whence Jonathon had disappeared... how long ago, perhaps ten minutes. She wondered how long it would be before he appeared there again, coming up, back to her, and what would have happened by the time he came. What the devil's the matter with me, she thought, why should anything have happened?

Outside there was a sudden scuffle of noise and a child's shout of laughter. The sound broke the nightmare and she drew a deep breath and straightened her shoulders. Something was pricking the back of her neck and she put up a hand to discover what it was. A sudden sharp pain in her third finger made her draw it back quickly. She stared at it in amazement. It was covered with blood.

"Yes," said the voice of the killer, "it is blood."

Before Elaine had time to react something slid past her face and she felt her arms pinioned to her sides.

"This knife," the ghastly whisper continued, and the killer's breath stirred the hair on Elaine's prickling scalp. "This knife is very sharp indeed. In fact so sharp that I feel sure you will agree to have a little talk with me. Not here, of course. That wouldn't do at all. Someone might come up, and I should hate to be disturbed. But we needn't worry that anyone will come. There's no one upstairs and we're going to have our little talk on the roof. I don't think anyone will trouble us up there, do you? And, of course, there's such a wonderful view. So long as one doesn't feel giddy of course…"

"Oh, no! I shouldn't try to shout." A hand was clamped over the girl's mouth while the point of the knife entered her skin between the ninth and tenth ribs. Elaine felt the warm trickle of blood crawling down her skin under her clothes…

In the empty hall the telephone's double peal rang on and on. Caroline heard it as she opened the cloister door and hurried in to answer it.

"Oh, Jonathan. Hallo, dear… Elaine? I doubt if she's in but I'll have a look." She put the receiver down and Jonathon on the other end of the line heard her footsteps fading away as she went off

to find the girl. Anxiety grew in him as the silence lengthened...
but it's absurd to worry, he thought, she's at home with her own
family... her own family! Oh God, no! that's madness. After a while
the footsteps returned, the receiver clanked as it was picked up
and he waited eagerly for Elaine's voice. But it was Caroline who
spoke. She sounded surprised but not alarmed.

"I'm afraid she's not here, Jonathon. Shall I ask her to ring you
when she comes in?"

"Well, no, actually I... Look, Mrs. Southey, may I come out and
wait for her with you? If you haven't seen her, you won't know,
but we went to see Grainger at the Yard this afternoon and he
said he'd be coming out to Magnolia House tonight. I don't know
whether he has any news... but, well, I'd like to be with Elaine,
if you don't mind."

"No, of course not. We shall be delighted to see you, Jonathon."

"Thank you, Mrs. Southey. I hope Elaine's all right... somehow
I can't stop feeling anxious about her."

Unreasonable as it seemed, Jonathon's anxiety was infectious,
and she went out into the street and looked up and down it. The
girl was nowhere in sight and she turned back along the cloister.
The street door banged behind her and she swung round to see
who had come in. It was William and the sudden sight of him
brought home to her how he had changed in this last week.

"Hallo, Caro, has something happened?"

"Well, no, it's Jonathon; he said something about having been
to Scotland Yard with Elaine this afternoon and for some reason
he was anxious because I didn't know where she was."

"Hmm. I wonder what took them to Scotland Yard..." His
manner changed abruptly. "I'd rather she was in. I'm going to
look for her."

Rather distractedly Caroline returned to the house. She unstrapped Desmond from his pram and carried him upstairs to the bathroom, taking comfort from the warm little cheek against her own. Only last week, she thought, we were getting ready for the party and nobody knew anything about Sweet being dead. Running the bath, undressing the baby, it was difficult to believe that the nightmare was real. "At least you don't know anything about it, darling," she said to the little boy. Her mind slid back twenty years to the memory of little Elaine at this age, and cold shivers of anxiety attacked her again. Jonathon ought to have told me why he was worried, she thought. What on earth had taken them to the Yard? Fear began to gain on her as she lifted the baby out of the bath with unaccustomed brusqueness so that he yelled his rage and indignation.

"There, boy, there," she murmured automatically. Why hadn't young Blake stayed with her if he was anxious, she thought indignantly? How were they to start looking for the girl when there was nothing to show them where to look? Surely William must be back soon. Even Richard was out. Oh God, she prayed, what do I do, what do I do now?

Outside on the stairway she heard Christine coming up for her bath. "Can I come in, Mummy?" she asked.

"Of course, darling," her mother called, trying to pitch her voice on a normal note. But the child asked at once, "What's happened?"

Before Caroline could answer the front door banged. "Oh, darling, run down quickly and see if that's Elaine," she instructed the child urgently and wrapping the baby in a towel she hurried down after her daughter.

"It's Dickey, Mummy," called Christine's voice from the hall.

"Oh…" Caroline hurried on down, watching her flying feet round the big baby in her arms.

"Oh, Dickey… you haven't seen Elaine, have you?"

"No, Mother, should I have?" Richard, radiant after a visit to an unwontedly welcoming Yolande in hospital, stared in distress at his mother's distraught face.

"No… no. It's just… Oh come up while I put Desmond down, will you, Dickey?"

"What is it, Mother, what's happened?" Richard asked when they were alone.

"Oh, Dickey, I expect… I hope it's nothing. I think I'm just in a panic… but Elaine doesn't seem to be anywhere and Jonathon thinks she ought to be here."

"Jonathon?"

"Yes, he rang up… Oh, Dickey, I'm so frightened."

"Poor Mummy," said Richard in distress. "Look, I'll put Dessie down, shall I, and then we can go into your room and you can tell me about it properly." He took the baby from her and put him in his cot.

"No," said Caroline, "he'll have to have something on, he'll get cold." She picked up a sleeping suit and put it on the little boy with trembling hands.

"There."

Richard drew her out of the nursery and sat her down in her own room with a cigarette.

"You smoke it, Mother, it'll do you good." He took one himself. "And now tell me exactly what has happened."

Caroline did her best to sound coherent and looked up at him questioningly.

"Yes, yes, I see." He inhaled, frowning. "She must have gone out again and it's ten to one that frightful woman next door will have noticed which way she went, she keeps her nose glued to the window-pane. I'll go and wring the truth out of her. Where's Father?"

"He went out to look for her."

A loud knock shook the front door, and with a startled look at his mother Richard raced down to open it, but Christine was before him. It was Jonathon.

"Where is she?" he demanded.

Richard motioned with his head at his mother standing on the stairs and answered quietly, "She's not come in yet. Mother's in a panic, don't you start. What the devil were you doing at the Yard today?"

Chris stood white-faced in the hall, looking at them.

"Come on, Jon," said Richard impatiently, but Jonathon shook his head. "I'd like to phone Grainger if you don't mind," he answered. "If he thinks there's nothing to worry about, then we can take our time. If he thinks she ought to be found, the police will do it faster than we will."

There was dead silence. Suddenly Christine began to cry.

"Oh, what's happened, why's everybody like this, where's Elaine?" she sobbed.

Caroline came down at once and took the little girl in her arms.

"Yes, Jonathon, I'd like you to ring the police," she said to him. "We'll be in the kitchen," and took Christine off with her.

After a brief conversation Jonathon put down the receiver. "Grainger'll be here in ten minutes," he said woodenly. "We're to stay where we are. He recommends that we keep together."

"All right, we'll do that in a minute," said Richard savagely. "But first, whatever anybody says, I'm going to talk to that woman next door. If Elaine went out again she will have seen her… if she didn't, we'll search the house. Go and tell Mother what's happening, will you?" he told Jonathon and slammed out of the house.

The sound brought Caroline from the kitchen. Jonathon explained as best he could. As they spoke footsteps sounded along the cloister. They listened painfully.

"It's William," said Caroline flatly. He came in, a haggard grey man, made of bone.

"I met Richard," he said.

Another pair of feet were coming round the corner of the house; William disappeared and after a moment they heard his voice.

"Oh hallo, Meade, no, no news yet. Very good of you to come…"

Richard rejoined them in a few moments, "The woman and the child are both out," he announced briefly. "Jonas says he hasn't seen her since five-thirty."

There was a silence, then William spoke to his wife:

"I know it's a hard thing to ask," he said so quietly that the others could scarcely hear him, "but I want you to take Christine in with Desmond and stay with them. As soon as there is any news I promise you shall know."

Caroline looked up at him. She took Christine by the hand and they walked slowly upstairs together.

William turned to where Richard, Jonathon and Meade stood waiting.

"I think we'll start in the basement," he said.

The police arrived before they had finished searching the unused cupboards and cellars that tunnelled away under the pavements.

They stood urgently on the doorstep, a group of dark-clothed men led by a Grainger so bleak that for a moment they didn't recognise him. Beyond them a movement in the garden suddenly caught Jonathon's eye and like a shot he was after it. A policeman followed close on his heels. But it was only the child Theresa climbing back into her own garden. He turned back to the house. He was no longer conscious of himself, of living, of having a mind. Only of two voices endlessly ringing in the empty cavern of his head. One said, "It can't be as bad as this!" and the other howled desperately, "Why did I leave her...? Why did I leave her...?" Suddenly he noticed something, without consciously registering what it was, and like an automaton he moved towards it. The policeman put a hand on his shoulder. "We're taking over now, sir," he said. Jonathon shook off the hand and walked on.

"It's a shoe," he said, "a woman's shoe." The policeman saw it, too. He sprinted ahead of Jonathon. Grainger got there a second later. He straightened up and said loudly:

"It's not Miss Southey's." He stood there a moment looking down at what he had found.

"Will you all wait inside, please," he said urgently then. "We'll let you know as soon as Miss Southey is found." And with McGregor behind him he raced upstairs.

As they reached the second floor they heard someone above them.

"Who's that?" asked Grainger sharply. "I told Anderson to keep them together."

Mac shook his head as he raced on. "Whoever it is he's got a guid start on us," he jerked out breathlessly.

They reached the attics and doubled through the intercommunicating rooms into the little cistern room behind. A ladder

led up on to the roof and they scrambled up it breathing hard. At
the top a door opened into blaring daylight. They climbed out and
scanned the roofs that surrounded them on every side.

"It's young Blake," said Mac suddenly.

"Look down there!" commanded Grainger grimly. He had
climbed astride the nearest pitch of the multiple roof and peering past his shoulder Mac saw a bundle in a green dress and short
white coat leaning face forward against one of the steep pitches
at the farther end of the roof, its feet resting on the edge below
which a hundred feet of brick wall stretched sheer to the ground.
Working his way around to the pitch on which Elaine lay was
Jonathon; his face was a white blur, his hair blowing wildly in the
wind that fluttered Elaine's clothing as she lay there, quite still.

"Sakes!" breathed the Scotsman hoarsely, but Grainger was
already lowering himself inch by inch across the ancient crumbling
tiles to the near end of the gutter above which she lay.

Jonathon was now leaning over the pitch above the inert
bundle that was Elaine. He peered down at her in an agony of
indecision. If he spoke or reached forward to touch her, she might
fall before he could get a firm grip. If once she started to slide
nothing could save her.

Suddenly he noticed Grainger close by her feet. The policeman shook his head and waved him back; he lay still, his eyes
desperately searching the huddle of clothes for signs of life. His
vision blurred under the concentrated strain and he raised his eyes
to re-focus them. Grainger was leaning towards the girl without
touching her, one hand gripping the tiles beside her. He was
looking down and back at his feet on the gutter; Jonathon raised
himself a little and understood why. Just beyond Elaine's pathetic
little feet in their high-heeled shoes a big piece of the broad leaden

conduit had broken loose and was hanging downwards. Though from his position he couldn't see it, he could imagine how the giddy drop must look through that yawning hole. Grainger placed his right foot on the edge of the gap and with his weight on the other, leant forward until his right hand, too, rested on the tiles beside the girl. At the same moment McGregor appeared astride the pitch on Jonathon's left. Grainger nodded at him briefly and mimed to Jonathon that he could speak now. With a prayer in his heart Jon leaned down towards her...

"Elaine...! Elaine...!"

The three men held their breath and watched. But there was no answering stir.

"Elaine!" Jonathon's voice was strangled as the attenuated thread of hope grew tauter.

"Elaine, my love, answer me!" In the windy silence that followed the older men heard a sob break from his throat.

And then it happened. Miraculously her head rose a few inches and above the gag that distorted the white face, her eyelids fluttered.

A sigh went over the watching men. Jon stretched out his hands and looked questioningly at Grainger who nodded vigorously. The young man edged himself forward.

"Don't... move... darling... please. Please don't move..." he breathed.

He had done it.

His hands were firm under her armpits. Assisted from below by Grainger, he drew her up on to the crest of the pitch and held her there, his arms about her like a vice.

Immediately all was bustle and activity; McGregor reached them first and his powerful fingers made short work of the gag and the rope that held her fingers pinioned. Above the cruel marks Elaine's face was grey, her eyes deeply shadowed. But her lids lifted and she stared at them.

"Darling, are you hurt? Show me where, sweetheart!" She shook her head weakly and a shudder went over her.

"She's icy cold—shock and exposure," said Grainger feeling her hands and face. He smiled at her with such sweetness that in other circumstances Jonathon would have been jealous, and said gently, "It's all over now. All over for good."

After a brief consultation they laid her tenderly across the broad back of the big Scot and roped her on safely. As if by common consent they all looked back at the gaping hole below them before they started back on their slow climb over the roofs to the waiting house within.

At last they dipped out of the cold wind down the ladder into the attics again. Inside the house it was dark and warm and blessedly still. They unstrapped her and laid her gently on the bed, wrapped in blankets, while Mac went off to tell her family. She lay with her head on Jonathon's lap, still unable to speak, while he stroked her forehead and massaged the sore muscles of her poor mouth.

Feet were pounding up the stairs and Jonathon leant back as Caroline dropped by the bedside and took her daughter in her arms.

# TWENTY

EVEN SO SOON THE MENACE, THE CORRODING BEASTLINESS that had haunted it had vanished from William's studio; the sparkling chandelier and the soft lights on the wide walls gleamed on rich pigments and soft brocades and on the pale faces of the seven people now gathered there among whom murder had dragged its bloody, destroying fingers for the eternity of seven days.

Paul Grainger gratefully accepted a chair and a drink and tobacco smoke rose in drifting grey coils against the light as pipes and cigarettes were luxuriously inhaled. Elaine's grey pallor had given way at last to a faint flush as she lay back on the model's couch wrapped in an eiderdown and Jonathon's protecting arm. Caroline sat in her own low chair and peace was in her face in spite of the marks of recent tears. Richard leaned against the wall, his young face older and sterner than a week ago, a hard look still settling on it when his eyes rested on the still livid gag marks about his sister's mouth. Old Henry Meade sat near him, his bald domed forehead resting on one blue-veined hand while he sucked with tired comfort at his silver-ringed pipe.

Sitting on the steps of the model's throne, William again faced Grainger; the painter was gaunt and pale, but his own particular vibrance had returned to him.

Caroline looked at the detective and said:

"It's only five days since you first sat there asking us how Ivan Sweet became our tenant and what we thought of him; it seems scarcely credible, even patently untrue, doesn't it?"

Paul Grainger smiled back at her. "Trying to believe something that felt patently untrue was one of my big problems in this case," he remarked. His eyes moved meditatively over the three young people. "For reasons you must understand," he continued carefully, addressing himself to William, "you and your wife were, with the possible exception of Patrick Sweet, my strongest suspects. On paper. But it felt patently untrue." His charming smile broke over his tired face.

"But, you see, as it turned out I was right. It *was* patently untrue. Perhaps you will allow me to say that it is very pleasant for me to sit in this room with you and know that I am not hunting a murderer amongst you." He sipped his drink, frowning a little with embarrassment, "I was particularly anxious to force my way through to the truth with all possible speed or I might have been under pressure to arrest you," he looked up at William and smiled wryly, "against my own conviction. I must confess that there were times when I wished it had been Ivan Sweet and not his killer that I was hunting."

William's penetrating gaze rested on the police officer. "I felt that you believed me," he answered simply. "What little courage I managed to muster in these last—incredible days rested on that sense, and"—he turned to Caroline—"on my wife's infinite generosity."

"I still don't really understand what happened," said Richard from the window. "Are we allowed to know now?"

Grainger looked at the young man gravely. "Yes. I don't see why you shouldn't," he answered. "I'll tell you." He leant his head back thoughtfully, his sandy lashes blinking as the bright light fell on his glasses.

"I don't think I need to tell any of you," he began, "that Ivan Sweet was an unlovable character and a blackmailer."

Caroline glanced rather anxiously at Elaine, Jonathon and Richard, but they appeared quite unsurprised. Grainger noticing the look smiled at her reassuringly.

"He had been a blackmailer, and doubtless an unlovable character as well, for a number of years; his own records suggest that he seriously began his career during the war... yes, he kept records, he was very methodical and kept a tally of profits made and notes of the evidence on which he levied them. He spent the war in successfully evading military, or any other form of service and kept himself, in part at least, by blackmailing the wives of soldiers fighting overseas, having persuaded these young women to sleep with him." He smiled wryly as he added, "I have been assured that Sweet was very attractive to women; as a mere man I can only be amazed! Despite these activities he seems to have been very poor at this time. Doubtless the frequent changes of address necessary to evade the police were a drain on his finances! He lived for a time in the East End where a Jewish grocer allowed him credit when he had no money. For this assistance to a stranger in time of need this unfortunate man was to pay dearly. He had no alibi for the morning of the murder and had been paying Sweet for his silence for ten years although these payments must have strained his resources; he, therefore, had to be added to my list of suspects.

"During the morning, then, besides your own family, Mrs. Moore and the Jonas's, all of whom could easily have made an opportunity to administer poison to Sweet, several other people who were involved with the case had been seen near the house.

These were, you, sir," he nodded at Henry Meade whose old eyes met his gravely, "the dead man's brother, Mr. Patrick Sweet, and another man who is I believe known to you, a Mr. Cecil Paignton. By the time I compiled this list I had, of course, had access to all Ivan Sweet's papers, including those he kept privately in a safe deposit. I realised that if the information given in these papers was correct all these people and the Jewish grocer, whose opportunity I was not then in a position to prove, had motives of varying strengths for wishing Sweet dead. My sergeant and I therefore concentrated on the checking of this information. As I had rather anticipated, it proved to be accurate. Thus everyone on the list had some sort of motive. There is, of course, nothing conclusive about the strength of a motive; people and their reactions vary greatly and one man may feel himself impelled to kill for a reason that seems inexplicable to someone else. But this doesn't mean, of course, that the commonest (and most understandable) motives, like the commonest diseases"—he smiled at Jonathon—"don't, in fact, occur most frequently.

"Up to this time, two points had particularly excited my curiosity. One was the method used by the murderer to introduce the poison to Sweet's drink—although the coffee and sugar were also possible vehicles, the accessibility of the cream, which stood for several hours in a pigeon-hole in the cloister, strongly suggested that this was the method used, particularly as the dead man seems to have rather advertised his habit of breakfasting on quantities of coffee and cream and was known to be a late riser. But I was curious to know what method the murderer might have used to introduce the poison with a minimum risk of observation. I decided that a hypodermic needle, carefully inserted into the cardboard lid at an angle would be the speediest and most efficient method. I was careful to broadcast this deduction, for if it proved to be true I hoped it would persuade the killer to try a little judicious planting of evidence. And, in fact, this happened, though we were able to solve the murder before we had time to go into this fully.

"While your family had"—he looked at William—"of all my suspects, the best opportunity to tamper with the cream in that it was natural for you to be in your own house on the morning when the poison was administered, there were a number of others who could also have had sufficient opportunity. I realised how many more when I studied the pigeon-holes in the approach. It is accessible to anyone and the cloister affords a good deal of privacy. Even if someone came round the corner from the house, it would be the work of a moment to slip through one of the arches in the wall and lie low until the ground was clear again.

"The other point that aroused my curiosity was related to the dead man's finances. He did not appear to earn any money, unless his blackmailing could be described under this heading," he added wryly; "these activities did indeed show a high rate of profit at times, still there seemed to me to be a discrepancy here. I was therefore not altogether surprised when I discovered that he had enjoyed a private income for some years past. I would not, however, have postulated gilt-edged securities bringing in nine hundred pounds a year."

A gasp went over the room. Jonathon voiced the general sentiment, "Do you mean to say he had all that money without working for it and yet spent his time blackmailing people to get more?"

Grainger nodded, a grim smile on his face. "It is incredible isn't it? I suspect that though he probably started it for money, later he did it for the pleasure it gave him."

William got up rather abruptly and went to his desk; he picked up a decanter and carried it round the room, pouring the golden brandy into the big-bellied glasses. The seven intent listeners, their attention momentarily diverted from the story of the killing, stirred, smelling the mixed smells of brandy and burning logs, oil-paints and turpentine; they remembered how delightfully ordinary life could be. The past and even the present seemed unreal. The moment, the hour, the day had no beginning and no ending, only a second-by-second significance.

"This inheritance," continued Paul Grainger in his quiet scholar's voice, "had not come to him from his own family, and I was curious to know how he had come by it. An idea did suggest itself to me; when I was making my initial search of his living-room, I found among his books some that did not belong with the rest. They were quite ordinary classics, very pleasantly bound in black leather with gilt edges, not because they were expensive books, but because they were old. Both the bindings and the novels themselves should have belonged to a Victorian lady, and, in fact, on the fly-leaf I found her! In faded, spidery characters was written the name, Mildred Price, and the date, 1892. Following up my hunch I set my sergeant to make a search among the wills at Somerset House. And it proved that Mildred Price had indeed bequeathed to Ivan Sweet the very comfortable private income he enjoyed. I kept this fact well lighted in my mind. It is difficult to over-emphasise the significance of money when investigating crime. We first ruled out any disgruntled Price relatives and I set in motion an intensive inquiry as to where and how Mildred Price and Ivan Sweet had met, and what had been their relationship. As I said before, money is always likely to be a storm centre. Naturally I was very interested to know how much Patrick Sweet, the dead man's brother, knew of Ivan's comparative wealth, for Ivan died intestate and Patrick is his next of kin. As you know, his family live on a sort of Bohemian starvation line, and he is in no very fit condition to fend for them. He hated and despised his brother and fratricide was an obvious possibility.

"This afternoon several things happened. First one of my men brought me in a very unwilling window-cleaner. He was the unappetising fruit of my inquiries into the relations between Ivan Sweet and Mildred Price. My man had done an excellent job in running this witness to earth after the period of years that had passed.

"He was a recalcitrant witness, but when we had calmed him down he told a reasonably clear story, in terms which suggested that the incident had (hardly surprisingly) stuck in his mind. He stated that he had been cleaning the windows of a big house in a London square, nine years ago, late on a winter afternoon, when he realised that something was tapping on the inside of the pane. He peered in, and in the dim light could just see a very thin old woman in bed. She was so thin and looked so strange that she made him feel 'spooky' he said. The light inside the room was very dim and he could only just pick her out. She was trying to raise herself with much painful effort and was tapping on the glass with her spoon. His first instinct was to move on to another window as fast as possible, but she was trying to say something, and after a moment he pulled down the window and stuck his head in to listen to the faint voice. There was, he said more graphically than I can, an offensive reek of sickness and the room was unbelievably untidy. He stared down at her, wondering if she was a lunatic and when she spoke, what she said seemed to confirm this suspicion.

"'Window-cleaner, you must get the police. I'm being poisoned, I made my will and he means to kill me, I know he does.'

"The window-cleaner muttered 'All right, Mum', and withdrew his head, carefully shutting the window. He had, as it happened, his own reasons for not wanting to contact the police at that time, and doubtless this biased his judgment. He did, however, spend a good deal of time and thought mulling over what he had seen and heard, and wondering what he should do about it. He even mentioned it to his girl, but she, knowing him to be a deserter, advised him to keep clear of the police. She produced the rationalisation which has quieted his conscience all these years, that if she was a loony as seemed probable, it was no kindness to her to send the police along."

Grainger knocked out his pipe and refilled it. "Since our inquiries had also brought to light the fact that Sweet had lived at this address for a while in 1947, this story naturally interested me very much. The questions I immediately asked myself were, of course, had Sweet been a murderer, and had someone tried to blackmail the blackmailer? I remembered an apparently irrelevant discovery I made here in your house, and it suddenly seemed highly relevant.

"At this point my attention was diverted by Patrick Sweet who walked into my room and confessed to the murder of his brother. He was very disturbed, I doubt if he had either eaten or slept for several days and he very much resented the questioning that followed his statement. That, in spite of his confession, we still found it necessary to *prove* that he had killed Ivan baffled and enraged him. He was not in a fit state to give a consecutive account of his movements and rambled on about his hatred of his brother, his family's need of the money and the fact that he possessed a hypodermic syringe. I received the impression that his decision to confess to the murder had momentarily relieved his pathological state of confusion, guilt and indecision. Actually the story he told did not fit in with the known facts and though I couldn't completely dismiss the possibility at that stage, I thought it unlikely that he was guilty of his brother's murder. However, I took advantage of the position to get him started on the psychiatric treatment he needs so badly.

"It was then that Miss Southey and Mr. Blake were announced. They brought me exactly what I had been looking for although I don't think they were aware of its significance in relation to the case." His eyes rested on them gravely. Taking his pipe out of his mouth he went on:

"It is at this point that I must tell you how bitterly I blame myself for not asking you whether you had confided your decision to talk to me; it was an unforgivable omission on my part and nearly led to tragedy." From the pocket of his suit he brought out a folded scrap of paper. "I know now from this note found on the body in the garden why you were in danger." His eyes sought Elaine's. "I imagine you left it before coming down to the Yard with Mr. Blake?"

"Yes," answered Elaine...

"Darling, you never told me about that..." interrupted Jonathon. "I had no idea you had done such a thing."

Elaine looked up at him contritely, "I'm sorry, darling, it never occurred to me. I was so pleased to see you and then we had to decide about going to the Yard, and there wasn't much time... I just forgot about it." Jonathon shook his head and tightened his arm about her.

"We know that the note represented merely a friendly warning to a defenceless woman, but the killer, very much on the *qui vive* and anticipating danger from every source by now, found it and interpreted it as a threat. If you try to imagine yourself into that state of mind, you will see that it could read either way according to the mind of the reader."

He handed the note to Elaine. She read it, frowning.

"Yes. Yes, I see now. I suppose it could have been. How amazing. It never occurred to me it could sound like that."

"Why should it?" replied Grainger gently. "I suppose when you came back she was waiting for you?"

"Yes," answered Elaine shivering. She frowned. "You know, I was scared stiff to come into the house. I stood out there after I'd said good-bye to Jonathon, trying to nerve myself to open the street door..."

"And yet you let me go!" exploded Jonathon. "Oh, darling, why, why didn't you tell me you were frightened?"

She smiled at him, "I wasn't... very... while you were there. It was after you'd gone. And anyway I thought it was just a silly feeling and I wasn't going to let it interfere with your work..."

"It doesn't occur to you that getting yourself all but murdered might interfere with my work! Oh, Elaine!" And regardless of watching eyes Jonathon buried his face in her hair.

There was a short silence. "Would you like to get it off your chest?" asked Elaine's father, "or would you rather forget all about it?"

"No. I'd rather tell you," Elaine replied after a pause; her voice was still husky after the long gagging.

"I was saying how I felt scared to go into the house, wasn't I? It was an extraordinary feeling, because we all love it so much, the house I mean. I looked up at it and it seemed to have changed its face; it was full of menace as if it meant to harm me." She shuddered suddenly as in imagination the bleak roofs wheeled round her again.

"I expect it was trying to warn you," remarked Richard suddenly. Elaine looked at him and Jonathon was amazed to see how, suddenly, the two looked alike.

"Yes," she said, "that was it, of course. Anyway," she went on after a pause, "I opened the door and went in. There was no one about. I walked slowly upstairs to my room, trying to shake off those beastly shivers of fright. When I got to the landing window I stopped there, looking out down the hill where Jonathon had gone and wondering how long it would be before I saw him climbing up it again. I was feeling a little better.

"It was then that I felt it, something pricking into my neck... and then... the voice spoke behind me... a ghastly hoarse whispering... and it all started..." She shivered and her eyes were haunted with horror.

"It's all over now, darling." Caroline was controlling her voice with difficulty. "Don't talk about it any more, sweetheart." Elaine shook her head.

"No," she said, "I'd like to, but I can't seem to think about it all clearly yet... I couldn't imagine what she was talking about, of course... it was a knife she had got and she had my arms pinned down and had gagged me with my own scarf before I had any idea what was happening... It all seemed so incredible, you know; I kept thinking later what a fool I'd been not to react more quickly while I had the chance, but when something like that happens to oneself it doesn't seem real... She kept asking me questions and making me go upstairs and then up the ladder... and then along the roof..." she laughed on a note of hysteria. "She said we were going to take a look at the view... I used to go up there quite a lot at one time... it's a wonderful view... but I never want to see it again... All the time the knife was pricking in between my ribs and the blood tickled as it ran down. I could feel her hating me so that I knew she wanted to push it right in... but... she didn't. I realised later if I'd been found with a knife wound it wouldn't have suited her, she wanted to do it but it wasn't what she'd planned.

"She asked me again and again, 'Who've you told?' Then she must have realised I couldn't answer anyway since I was gagged and she let out a horrible laugh and pulled it off with a jerk as if she wished it would break my neck. And she started again, 'Who had I told?' I said 'Told what?' and she laughed again in that ghastly way and said, 'Don't play the innocent with me. It's too late for that.' I didn't answer because I didn't know what to say and she shrieked furiously, 'Why did you have to interfere, you bloody little fool? He was a killer! Ah, you didn't know that, did you? He killed an old woman for her money and he tried to kill me! I tell you it wasn't murder; it was self-defence!'

"If I hadn't been so scared, I think I'd have begun to understand then, but I didn't. We were walking along those leaden conduits right on the edge and I knew they were full of rotten patches and I was trying to remember which were the worst bits... Then she started again, shrieking at me so that I hoped wildly that perhaps someone might hear her, but we were so high that the wind carried it all away, 'Who've you told?' she yelled, and when I still didn't understand she suddenly burst out as if she couldn't stand my stupidity any longer, 'That I killed Ivan Sweet, of course, you bloody little idiot!'

"I was so startled that I stopped, up to then I'd just assumed she'd gone horribly mad, but now I understood. She bumped into me and we both nearly went over. She swore and then asked me again, 'Well, who've you told?' And I answered truthfully, 'I haven't told anyone. I had no idea it was you who killed him.'

"I think she must have realised at that moment that I was telling the truth, for she stopped pushing the knife into my back and we both stood there while she thought it out. After a bit she said in a different sort of voice, 'Well, it's too late now, you'd have me hanged. You *know*.' 'But I won't say anything,' I said desperately, 'he was a dreadful man, I'm glad he's dead, he's done enough harm. I swear I'll never tell anyone!'

"I was trying to look at her over my shoulder; I thought if I could only look her in the eyes she'd see I was telling the truth. I hadn't seen her face until then, she'd been behind me all the time, and I... it looked horrible... all bone, and skin, and terrible eyes. I could scarcely recognise her. She didn't speak for quite a long time. And then she said, 'Oh yes, you will, you'll tell all right when you see your precious father about to hang for it!'

"I suppose my horror must have shown on what she could see of my face twisted over my shoulder. After that I knew there was no more hope unless I could somehow get the knife away from her, but she forced me along the gutter towards the far corner and the rope was so tight on my wrists I couldn't get my hands free. She was muttering to herself, 'If you go over here,' I heard her say, 'you'll fall into the garden. They'll find you too soon there, I shouldn't have time... it's got to be in the gully, they won't see your body there.'

"It was so bad by then I didn't seem to be frightened any more. I even laughed at myself for picking my way so carefully, avoiding the bits I knew were rotten. I missed a chance then, though, while I was looking down at my feet she got the gag on me again. After that I could only think I ought to have screamed while I had the chance. It all seemed to go on a very long time; I was so dizzy I wondered if I'd go over before she was ready to push me... and my head was full of pictures… of Jonathon and how it felt when we looked at each other… and little Dessie the day Mummy brought him home from hospital… and how I'd longed to have a baby of my own one day… and things Dickey and I used to do when we were children… Oh, all sorts of things seemed to be spinning through my head. But I knew we were getting nearer and nearer to the corner by the gully. It seemed as if years and years went by as we drew nearer and nearer to it…

"Then it all happened so suddenly that I didn't understand at first. I heard a rending sound, and I thought automatically, that's rotten wood. There was a sort of gasp and suddenly the knife wasn't pushing into my back any more; I stayed quite still and I don't know how long it was before I made myself turn round. There was a little cloud of powdered wood-dust drifting out round the gutter beside me. When at last I did turn round there was no one behind me any more, only a big piece of gutter hanging downwards by its leaden covering. I thought quite automatically that one of the modillions must have gone. We've always been afraid one of them would go, haven't we… I suppose that one saved my life by breaking when it did… I stood there looking at the gap and I began to feel all dizzy. I managed to turn round so that I shouldn't have to look down and I remember seeing the line of the pitches above me swinging up and down as if there were an earthquake and I laid my face on the tiles and I think I must have gone right out for a while because later I came to and couldn't think where I was or why it was so bitterly cold. When I remembered, I tried to climb up the tiles so that I could get up on to the pitch away from the edge, but my arms were tied and I kept getting fresh waves of dizziness… You know the rest," she ended.

There was a silence. Then Richard burst out:

"She must have been mad! I can't think why we didn't realise it."

"No," said Grainger slowly, "Naomi Moore wasn't mad. But she had that inflexible quality of selfishness that you will find in nine murderers out of ten. It's a moral, not a mental lack. One she shared with the man she killed."

"But why did she have to kill him?" persisted Richard. "Couldn't she have protected herself by turning him over to the police?"

"Yes, that's the way the normal mind works." Grainger picked up his drink and swirled it absently. "She hadn't the normal person's faith in or solidarity with the forces of law and order, but she must have considered the possibilities of that before she decided that he must die. I think she realised that there wasn't sufficient evidence to hang him for the murder of Mildred Price. And she wouldn't have been safe unless she could be sure of getting him under lock and key. He had twice tried to kill her, remember. Those 'accidents' you came to tell me about today were no accidents, of course. They were very ingenious murder attempts. I had already been puzzled by traces of a tripwire before I heard about them. No one knew better than Naomi Moore how ruthless Sweet could be. They were not dissimilar and probably recognised this; they both possessed a highly unpleasant gift of inspired curiosity about other people's affairs and they specialised in skeletons in cupboards. But while Sweet meticulously proved and docketed his information, much of which he got through her, and turned it into money, she was content with the sense of power her inspired guesses afforded her." He smiled grimly as he added, "But when her nose led her to Mildred Price, the little old woman who had had money and no one to protect her, the time began to draw near when 'curiosity must kill the cat!' It was inevitable, when these two ghouls turned their weapons against each other, that one of them would be destroyed. What they didn't foresee was that it would end in their mutual destruction."

There was a silence in the room until Caroline said in her soft voice:

"How terrible that two people should have died, and that one feels—glad—that they are dead."

Her epitaph on his case still sounded in Paul Grainger's ears as he stood in the wide doorway of the hall with Caroline and William some time later. The three of them stood in the dark looking out over the threshold that had seen nearly three hundred years of family life. Already the shadow of death and violence was passing and a mist with an autumnal tang hung over the quiet garden, sharpening the scents of flowers dimly guessed in the faint starlight.

"Caro and I will go away for a little… for our second honeymoon," William's voice was quiet in the darkness; "when we return, I hope you will come again, not on duty, but in your free time."

On the faces turned towards him Grainger saw their warm smiles in the dim light; through the fog of fatigue that enclosed him he felt himself moved by their friendliness.

"I will," he said.

THE END

*The previously unpublished poem that follows is
not part of* Scandalize My Name, *but is included
here, as a coda of sorts, by kind permission of the
estate of Fiona Maud Peters.*

# BEQUEST

These beauties that have lit my eyes
These songs my melting ears remember
These soul-conquering fragments that roar
From man's long past with glory
In our exploring minds, this glittering
Crusade my thoughts have danced and fought upon,
This spangled air round whose necessity
Wheel eternally the holy sparks of life,
These emerald spears that yearly thrust
Through our blind earth's unlikely crust,

These ephemeral petals whose colours sing
A new Messiah spring by spring,
These enchanted fragments of all living things
That bear unknowing
The trademark of eternity;
These wits that build and wound, enslave and free
Our half-blind, half-seeing
Trembling and proud humanity,
This tenderness that makes our hands
The loveliest of all fleshly things,

This love that like the universe
Eternally expands our light-thirsty
 Souls; my little share of these
 I now bequeathe; for death has marked me out
 And but by his lingering courtesy
 This heart still beats, these lungs expand,
 These bitten bones support
. This once-proud frame, the round flesh
 Already lopped here where his claws have touched,
 A monster's foretaste of the feast that waits,

 My warm blood cooling, my quick limbs stilled,
 My eye's soft lustre dark and dumb:
 Yet helpless as I am I'll tell
 Dark death he is no more than bright
 Life's shadow, life's and love's counterpart;
 Procreative fingers are not his,
 Nor love's warm-breathed eternity;
 All his harvest only hungers him
 Who can only take, but never make
 One living thing.

FIONA PETERS

JANUARY 1961.

## ALSO AVAILABLE
## IN THE BRITISH LIBRARY
## CRIME CLASSICS SERIES

Many of our titles are also available
in eBook, large print and audio editions